Cuckold Stories

Angelina Moore

Cuckold Stories

Cover design by: Angelina Moore

For questions and suggestions:

ashinaverlag@gmail.com

Edition 2022

CONTENT

HER FIRST TIME

She's late, and I already know why. With the phone off, without a word, without even a short text, I know.

The dinner I cooked is cooling on the table in front of me; the dinner I know I told her I was cooking for us, a special for tonight. I reach for my phone and try to call again, but pause briefly, my hand hesitating, shaking slightly, before dropping back to my lap.

I know why.

I wonder who he is; someone from work or the gym? How does she know him? Does she even know him, or maybe this time it's a complete stranger? My hands fidget on my lap, my nails tugging at my cuticles, I feel my chest rise and fall with the machinations of my mind.

Is he taller than me? Is he in better shape? Probably; and
I don't even have to wonder if he's taller than me,
because I know he must be.

Just like the last time. The last time she came home
flushed and breathless, an energy and a vibrancy in her
eyes that I hadn't seen in nearly a decade of marriage.
Back then, she barely walked in the door before she
pressed her lips to mine.

I could taste it clearly on her lips. A calling card; a
lingering sign of her dalliance, adding an extra sheen to
her swollen and red lips, a new dimension to her breath.
It had burned when she had seen the look of shock and
discomfort on my face as I tasted another man on her
breath. Again, that urgent and hungry look that I hadn't
been able to give her for some time.

She had dropped her clothes, right there in the living
room. Her shirt fluttered off her shoulders, her breasts
bra-less.

She made me pull down her panties, and I swear she
was shaking as I gasped, not knowing what I had done.
They had been soaked, soaked with her juices that had
clearly mixed with his. A lingering imprint of another

man leaking copiously from my wife's most private place to stain her panties. Her lips, waxed completely clean then and for the first time I saw them, were swollen and red; red to match the pink marks and bruises on her inner thighs where he had pressed against them, where his skin had marked her skin when he had fucked her. When he had fucked my wife.

I had no words, only shame mixed with a heady, thrilling, drug-like arousal that gripped me furiously. My eyes were glued to her swollen, sticky pussy lips, from which his cum was still leaking. I had watched it slowly drip in long, viscous drops from her well-fucked hole to the soaked panties that had been pulled halfway down her thighs.

I felt her trembling as I knelt breathlessly before her, eyes fixed on the brazen evidence of her experience; her sexual experience, without me. I had felt her hands on my head, clutching my hair as she stood trembling before my stricken and heavily breathing face. She had said nothing in the heavy silence of the room, but the urgency in her grip, the ever-so-slight tugging of my head toward her, said it all.

I don't know why or how it happened then. That part was nothing we had ever talked about, nothing either of us had even imagined. But there I was, on my knees, letting her pull my mouth to her cum-soaked pussy, from which dripped another man's seed.

I hear the garage door open, the familiar sound of her car. I tense my jaw, a cold yet charging sensation racing through my veins. Now; now my burning questions will receive answers.

The opening of the side door is a familiar sound, as is the metallic clank of her keys hitting the tray on the door; all routine, all normal. Knowing where she's been and what she's been doing and what's probably dripping and leaking from her pussy right now, though, is new.

"Honey?

I swallow hard, my hands still fidgeting on my lap as my heart hammers in my chest. My cock is rock hard.

"I'm... I'm in here." My voice trembles, cracks slightly. The warm tide of shame and excitement creeps up my face.

She enters, drops her purse on the chair by the door, and stops in the doorway. I close my eyes and swallow again before slowly opening them and lifting them to meet hers.

Her hair is a mess; disheveled and wild and hastily tied back from her face. Her normally flawless and exquisitely applied makeup is anything but flawless; her eye shadow is heavier than normal and smudged, her lipstick smeared across her lips. But it's that look in her eyes-that wild, vivid, hungry look-that pierces me and makes my heart flip and my stomach clench.

"Oh..." She starts, her eyes darting quickly over the tabletop filled with cold food between us. "I, uh, forgot." She gives me a quick, apologetic look, like this is any old name, like she's stuck in traffic.

"That's okay." My voice feels strained and forced. I can barely hear my own words as my pulse pounds in my ears.

"I just...I got caught up..." She trails off, her wild and lustful eyes straying back to stare into mine, making me feel small.

"Sorry." She doesn't look it.

"No, no, it's okay." The questions feel pent up behind my lips, overlapping and threatening to fall out all at once in a huge, incomprehensible vomit.

"I can warm it up." She looks at me again; is that pity in her eyes? I drop my eyes to her and notice the wrinkles in her blouse, the missing button, the way her full and perky chest rises and falls violently as if she's just climbed a flight of stairs.

I can feel the tension rising, the questions crying out for relief as she casually acts like this is just another night.

"I....where..." She begins to stumble now, the words, the questions crashing through the damnation slipping past my mouth.

Suddenly she grins at me; a wicked, knowing smile on her face, a fire in her eyes.

" You want to know where I've been, don't you". She says it coolly, without question and with a grinning humor in her voice.

"Yes!" ... I practically yell it. The blood roars in my ears from barely contained arousal, and my erection tugs at the front of my pants.

She just smiles at me; this time she's going to pull it out.

"I bet you want to know everything, don't you, baby?" She bites down on her bottom lip as her mouth curls into a maroon grin. God, I can picture her with that same look, dropping her panties for whoever she was with.

"Oh God, yes, baby!" I beg; of course I beg....

Her eyes light up like fire as they stare into mine, and she slowly begins to unbutton her cardigan. She shrugs and drops it on the floor.

"What do you want to know?" She winks at me.

"Everything!" My cock is painfully erect in my pants, and I realize my white-knuckled fingers are clutching the edge of the dining room table as I hang on her every word.

She winks at me, shakes her head, and wags her finger. "Uh, uh, honey. One question at a time answered. Her cheeks are flushed, her wild, tousled hair framing her face.

"Who..."

"Franz, from work." She finishes for me.

I feel the floor fall out from under me and my stomach flips. Franz! She works with him! I had met him! The guy is a stud; tall, big shoulders, arms like a fighter. I remember meeting him at the Christmas party in her office. He had shaken my hand and made a joke about my lackluster grip. The women around him, my wife included, had laughed at the joke as I had blushed and tried completely in vain to come back with anything; all I had found were mumbles.

Later that night, he had bragged to me about screwing his eighteen-year-old secretary while we were both at the urinal. He had clapped me on the shoulder as I tried to squeeze piss through my clenched bladder, completely shy of hearing his powerful stream just moments before he thundered into the porcelain beside me.

"Good luck, little guy." He had said with a laugh, before making me grit my teeth and try in vain to loosen my bladder.

"Yeah, honey, you met him."

She starts walking toward my chair from the dining room doorway.

"He was in the parking garage after work." She moves slowly toward me now as she unbuttons the front of her rumpled and wrinkled blouse one button at a time.

"He helped me carry some files to the car. And he's so charming." She pauses at her blouse and grins at me,

"Well, you know that, you've met him." Her fingers undo another button.

"Anyway, he's always so flirty with me - oh, did I mention that? - Yeah, he's always very affectionate, very flirtatious with me. Anyway, we were alone in the parking lot, and he was behind me when I bent down to put the files in the trunk, and before I knew it, his hand was on my butt!

The blood rushed to my face, all over my body, as I thought about how this man, this big alpha cop I met, put his hand on my wife. She is standing right next to me now, shrugging her blouse off her shoulders. I realize how fast I'm breathing now, hanging on her words.

"Well, I knew I should be angry, honey; I knew I should say no to being married, but..." She pulls back as her fingers trail over the perfect skin on her hips and reach back to unhook her bra.

"But really, I wanted his hand there. I wanted a big stud of a man to want me so badly that he put his hands on me even though he knew I was another man's.

Her bra comes off and falls from her shoulders. Her dark and erect rosy nipples flash and I inhale sharply; he left marks. Bruises and reddened red hickeys from another man's mouth cover my wife's perfect breasts.

"Instead, I turned around and kissed him, honey". Her fingers wander over her breasts, over his love bites there as she speaks. Her face is flushed and she has a glow about her; the glow of having been fucked fresh and senseless by another man.

She looks down at my lap with a grin. "You can take it out, baby."

My hands are still locked on the tabletop. In a flash, they yank on my belt and zipper.

She giggles, " Always in such a hurry..."

Crimson floods my cheeks, and I pull slowly and manically on my zipper. She shakes her head and looks at me like I'm some kind of disobedient child.

"Anyway, we made out like teenagers, honey. His mouth was all over my neck, and his big, strong hands felt so good on my body! God, he's so strong! Before I knew it, he had me pressed up against the side of the car, my shirt and bra off."

My zipper is down and my hand is inside fishing for my painfully hard little cock.

"I could feel his huge cock pushing into me through his pants, and - oh, baby - I just had to have it; it felt so big!". She moans slightly now as her fingers find the zipper on the side of her skirt and begin to pull it down.

"It was so primitive, honey, I wanted him so bad; needed him. I took off his belt and pulled down the zipper - oh, go ahead baby, just pull it out".

I pulled my very hard, very medium sized cock out through my fly while listening with rapt attention and a hot feeling in my belly. I moan and think of my wife fingering this other, bigger, stronger man with a huge cock in the parking lot while I cooked her dinner at home!

"I had to have him, had to have that cock! So I got down on my knees, baby, and pulled on his zipper. He wasn't wearing any underwear, and his cock just flew out of his pants; and it was fucking huge!"

Her eyes closed as she said it, and she pulled her lower lip between her teeth. Something like a moan comes out of her mouth, and she lets the skirt fall to the floor and float to her feet. Suddenly I gasp and hold my erection tightly in my fist: there, where her thighs meet, is a huge wet spot covering the crotch of her lacy blue panties. Blood roars in my ears; is.... is this from him? Is it her own desire? Probably both!

She sees where my eyes are glued and giggles; "Oh, I'm getting to that, darling".

Then she starts to move and walks around behind me. "Well, Franz's cock was absolutely gigantic, honey; a really thick monster. I was almost scared of it the first time it fell out of his pants! I could barely grab him with two hands; I probably could have used a third hand! He was so hot, so thick in my little hands, that I immediately got wet just holding such a huge cock."

She leaned against my ear from behind; "he was at least three times your size, honey". I moaned and felt shame wash over me, knowing that I was no match at all for this bull of a man. My cock jumps into my hand and I stroked it faster.

She starts to pull my chair away from the table again. I felt so stupid that I pulled my average cock out through the zipper of my pants while she pushes my chair back for me.

" Did you...did you..."

"Did I blow him?" Her voice coming from behind me, her lips almost touching my ear, and I moaned at the sensation

"Yes, baby, I did! I was so aroused just feeling the weight of him in my hands that I just threw myself on him! I could barely get my head between my lips; I didn't even know my jaw could open that wide."

Now she's walking around the chair, moving between
my chair and the table. She grins wickedly at me as she
leans back against it.

"So did I give him a blow job? No, honey."

I felt some of my shock dissipate; she hadn't done it!
Had they just made out?

"No, a blowjob is what I'm doing to you, honey; a job.
Her evil grin returned. "No, I didn't give Franz a
blowjob..." She leans toward me, her breasts swaying as
she leans in close, sitting wide-eyed and barely breathing.

"I let him fuck my face."

My breath catches in my throat at her words, and I
squeeze my painfully hard cock erratically. She giggles
and leans back.

"Oh, honey, a man like that just deserves to take what
he wants. Your little wife must have looked like such a
dirty whore on her knees in the parking lot while she

allowed another man to use her mouth like that! I could hardly stand it! He held my hair in his hands and fucked my lips like a pussy, so all I had to do was gag and drool and drool all over his huge, fat cock."

She scoots back and hops up on the dining room table, pushing my cold food away as she leans back and opens her legs in front of me.

Her hands are now at the front of her soaked and dirty panties, rubbing at the wet spot, pulling the material tight against her mound and sliding the damp material over her slickly waxed labia.

"Honey, I was so aroused too, I could have just come from gurgling on his monster cock". Now she's rubbing harder through her soaking wet panties, the material making squeaking noises as she consciously moves her fingers in circles, panting.

"I had my skirt rolled up around my waist while he fucked my throat, and I played with my pussy while he did it," she gasps as her fingers blur over the soaked panties.

"I was such a slut to him, baby. Your wife was another man's whore, on her knees in a parking lot, letting him use her mouth!

I watch her with rapt attention as she moans, eyes closed, imagining this other man's huge fat cock as I wildly stroke my average erection. My eyes are riveted to the sodden gusset of her panties, soaked with what I'm now sure is a huge load of Franz's cum.

"He came in my mouth, baby." It comes out almost like a gasp, like a whisper from her lips, and I moan.

"He filled me full and I swallowed every drop of it. Oh, I know, honey. I know I usually like to spit it out when I suck you off. But his cum tasted so good, and I was so turned on, I loved sucking it down. It was such a rush!"

I gasp and stroke my little red cock as I watch her play and listen to her tell me how she let another man do something to her and treat her like she never let me.

"And then... Did you come home?"

She laughs loud and hard, and her eyes open to meet mine with a fiery eagerness.

"Oh... goodness, no! Of course not honey, there was so much more. Would you like to hear what happened next?"

"Yes!" I croak it out, desperation in my voice. She giggles.

"Well, he was still rock hard after he shot his load down my throat. I know we... You're having trouble with this, honey, but he definitely isn't. You see, he's a real man, a real stud with a big cock".

"He pulled me up and pushed me over the hood of the car, right there in the parking lot! He took his shirt off, and his muscles are so yummy, baby. He really works out!"

She notices me starting to reach for my shirt and she giggles, "Oh.... no, that's ok, just leave it on, honey". I ignore the sting in my pride, knowing I haven't gone to the gym in years, and drop my hand back down to the throbbing erection sticking out of my pants.

"He had me on my back on the hood of my car, my legs pushed up to my chest. Oh, he's so strong, honey. He held me so that my skirt was pushed up around my waist, and he..." Her fingers just slide under the edge of her cum-soaked panties, and she starts to pull them to the side.

"He just pushed my panties out of the way as he fed his huge cock to this little pussy!".

Her wet panties are pushed aside, and I gasp and moan as she exposes herself to me as she sprawls out in front of me on our dining room table. Hers - my wife's - pussy is red and sore; swollen and still stretched from the fucking it received at the hands of another man. I moan, a whimpering sound, and my cock wags as I watch the glob of sticky white cum ooze from her cunt as she spreads her red and waxed labia with her fingers.

She grins at me, "Oh, no, of course we didn't use a condom, honey. Condoms are only for little crippled husbands; only real men can go in naked and fill my pussy with their cum.

Her words drive me crazy, my cock wiggling in my fist as I grip it tightly, stroking it madly to the dirty, erotic thoughts of my wife being fucked rough by this big alpha bull of a man.

"I thought he might be too big, baby; his cock was really great, bigger than anything I've ever seen! Well, bigger than anything I've seen since I married you".

I moaned.

"Oh, he stretched your wife's pussy wide, baby. He had to really dig in, but I was so wet he filled me all the way. I could feel his huge cock in places I've never felt your cock before," she moaned. Her fingers squeezed into her sticky, dripping folds and masturbated before my eyes, using another man's cum to slide her fingers over her clit and between her labia.

"He fucked me hard and deep, holding my legs back and wide and just pounding me and using my little pussy". Her fingers are buried in her red, raw and gaping pussy making loud wet noises as she fucks herself. Her eyes are closed again, and I know it's the possessed stud who fucked her while I was home, and she imagines herself enjoying herself.

"Did...did you come?" The words tumble out of my mouth in a rasping whisper. I flinch furiously now, so close because I wanted to come so badly.

She laughs, a mocking, harsh sound. "Oh, dear, of course I did! How could I not? I know it takes some work on you, but as it turns out, a big fat cock stretching my little married pussy like that gets me in all the right places! I lost track baby, I came so many times on that big hard cock of Franz".

My fist moves over the throbbing head of my cock. My hand is almost completely gripping my cock, and I'm even trying to imagine having something as big as Franz between my legs.

"At some point he even reaches underneath and grabs my ass with one of his fingers, honey! I know we've never done this before, but I think next time, and yes honey, there will be a next time, I'll let him fuck my ass."

I gasp and start to sputter, my erection suddenly losing some steam. Your ass!? That's something we never talked about!

"But! But we never... I mean, we never talked about..."

"Oh, honey," she looks at me pityingly, her face beginning to crumple as her fingers squeeze loudly in and out of her well-fucked hole.

"It doesn't matter what we talked about anymore because I belong to Franz now," she says. She begins to pant, her eyes closing as she finger fucks her cum filled pussy. Her wedding ring glistens wetly in the dining room light.

"I'm his slut now, dear, and he can do whatever he wants with me. I'll be his whore".

I'm hot and cold all over at the same time, with a leaden, sickening feeling in my belly. And yet my cock is wiggling, rock hard in my hand. I start stroking again, thinking of my wife serving this big-tailed stud and being his whore.

"Yes, honey, Franz is going to - oh God! - use me... anytime... - Oh! - he wants to! And there's - ah! - nothing you can do about it!"

She climaxes with a loud cry, her whole body tensing as she imagines the other man's big cock fucking her every which way. God, she's so fucking beautiful.

"Okay." I barely exhale as I stroke my raging hard cock. It's the only word that comes to mind.

Gasping for air, she slowly opens her eyes and looks at me lovingly. "Oh, I knew you'd understand, baby." She looks down at my cock and realizes I'm still stroking and haven't come yet.

"Oh... I... you haven't come yet?"

I shake my head, my eyes wide. I wish for her so badly right now.

My wife just smiles at me. "Here, darling." She gets up from the table and slides her soaked and cum-soaked panties down her legs. She drops them wetly into my lap, and I gasp in shock as they land on my cock.

"They're already oiled up for you, honey. Why don't you just take them to make you come, ok?". She says it sweetly, but with something dark and fiery in her eyes.

"But aren't you..." I stumble over my words, and she just smiles at me.

"Oh, no, honey, I'm going to go heat up dinner. But why don't you just go ahead?"

With a quick kiss on the cheek, she leaves the room for the kitchen.

With a small, suppressed moan, I wrap her sticky panties, soaked with another man's cum, around my cock.

And I begin to stroke.

HUSBAND WATCHES

The rage swirled up inside me every time. No matter where I was or what I was doing. The thought of him. That he was touching her. My wife.

The rage always seemed to be waiting to assault me. And no matter how many times it happened, I was never prepared for it.

As I stood on the altar, looking down the aisle at her while everyone we knew crowded into the cathedral with us, I could only think of one thing.

"Let it go," he said.

The spiteful laughter poured out of me. "Let it go?I'm paying you a thousand euros an hour for that? A Disney cartoon platitude?" As I stood up, I glanced around the therapist's ostentatious office with diplomas hanging on

the walls boasting of his accomplishments.
Accomplishments of what? Just for passing this or that
school?

A big fucking deal.

By the time he was studying for midterms, I had
dropped out of college and started my own software
company. It was so easy for me. It was accounting
software! Fucking math! A kid could do that.

As I walked across the room, I wanted so badly to
punch him. Just punch him in the bearded face and
finish him off. But I didn't. No matter how much
money I made, I was still the little nerd that everyone
picked on. Money and success were supposed to be my
revenge. But it was so hollow.

My money undoubtedly helped me land my dream girl,
Maria. She wouldn't have looked twice at me if it weren't
for my success. She never would have gone to bed with
me, that's for damn sure.

Unfortunately, I wasn't her first. She had been with
others before me. Three I was sure of. And three others
I suspected. None since we met, and certainly none

since we married. She would never cheat on me, and I would never cheat on her. I really love her, and I believe deep down that she loves me.

Everyone I knew, and many who didn't made it clear that I was a fool to marry her without a prenup. Why would I do that? I would answer them. Why should I trust her with my whole life and not my money?

By all accounts, we lived a perfect life. And we did. Except for one thing I never got over. My overwhelming jealousy. Jealous of those who had sex with Maria before me.

My jealousy was so great that I wanted to kill my therapist just because he knew about her past. He knew about Maria's past because I had told him, and that still made me angry. I wanted to hit him just so he wouldn't remember. So he couldn't giggle about my wife behind my back with his friends. About how many men had been with her. In front of her nerdy little husband.

"You've tried everything else to overcome this problem, haven't you?"

I glanced out the window at the growing city skyline. "Just about." I said.

"Have you tried to do just the opposite?"

Maria was a beautiful, blonde swimsuit model. She was passed over by Sports Illustrated for their idiot photographer. I suspect he was hitting on Maria during a topless shoot. When his advances were rejected, he took it out on her through the photos. Maria never said anything to me about it. She even insisted that I not participate in her photo shoots because of my angry outbursts.

When I got home from the therapist, I saw that she had just come home from a workout. Even all sweaty, she looked amazing. Her skin-tight yoga pants tempted me almost as much as her big, round breasts in her tank top.

She led me through the house as she headed for the shower. For a moment, I thought of her as a pied piper. But then I realized he was leading rats. To their deaths.

In her huge bathroom (it was bigger than our old living room where we grew up), she lifted her white top over her head, revealing her blue sports bra. She glared at me, knowing I liked to watch.

She pushed her breasts unnecessarily through the bra fabric, just for my benefit. I appreciated that very much. Then she slowly peeled down her yoga pants.

As I watched her strip for me, I thought about the therapist's ridiculous plan. Maria was so beautiful and I loved her so much, but something had to change. My jealousy was ruining my life.

Maria bent down in front of me to take off her socks. Her pretty, perfect ass was parted by her wet and cock stiffening slit.

That beautiful ass was all mine, but anger was starting to creep in. Six guys were sticking their rock hard cocks inside Maria. Right there. Right in her tight little cunt.

I reached out with my fingertips and grazed her bare ass. She spun around and playfully slapped my hand away. "I know you like to watch," she said to me. "Watch me shower and then we'll play."

She smiled at me and the anger melted away. The relief
that she was mine felt wonderful after the anger. If only
I could keep that feeling all the time.

The therapist was right, nothing had worked. Time to
try something new. Even though the thought of it
nauseated me.

Maria let the steaming water pelt down on her. The
rivulets flowed over her naked body. Down from her
shoulders, over and between her full breasts, down her
flat stomach and over her mound, then filtering through
her tiny dark pubic hair.

She was right. I loved to watch. Watching her was like
watching my own Playboy channel. Standing in front of
the shower with my pants down, I stroked my hard
cock. Of course, I never had sex as a teenager. Jerking
off in front of beautiful women was one of my favorite
pastimes. Only now I was having my very own.

She had barely dried off when we made it to the bed.
Her skin and hair were still damp, but she smelled so
clean and fresh.

She lay on her back while I wedged myself between her legs. Missionary style was my favorite. I could see everything and I was in control.

Unfortunately, my control was not great.

I rubbed my cock against her wetness before she reached down and guided me inside. She hummed with pleasure as I entered her. I started thrusting back and forth, and she was so beautiful, and I kept pumping, and she closed her eyes and moaned and....

I lost control and came inside her. When I had pumped my last bit, I collapsed in her arms. As always, she held me tight and asked if I was okay. I was.

"Was it good for you?" I asked her, as I always do.

She smiled and nodded as she bit her lower lip. "It was fantastic," she said, "May I finish?"

"Of course not," I said on my cue to get out of her way. "Go ahead. Do your thing."

She reached into the drawer on the nightstand and pulled out her new toy.

Even though I was spent, I watched in anticipation as Maria pulled out a massive black cylinder. It was a new one and much larger than any of the others.

She grinned at me as she ran it along her body.

Jesus Christ, I thought. Look at the size of that thing. It looked like a goddamn table leg.

She stroked it against her pussy and clit. Then she closed her eyes and put it between her thighs.

Watching her pleasure herself awakened lust in me again. My cock started to get hard again. It was quite a remarkable recovery.

Maria's lips pursed as a slight moan escaped. She eased the cylinder inside her back and forth with one hand. With the fingers of the other hand, she massaged her clitoris.

Deep inside me I felt satisfaction that my beautiful wife was enjoying this pleasure.

I began to stroke myself. As I looked down at myself. I suddenly felt stupid. My cock looked insignificant. It was ridiculously small compared to her new toy. I was pathetic.

A burning sensation rose in my face, and I recognized it immediately. I was ashamed. Humiliation.

There I was, naked in bed, and my gorgeous wife was playing with herself while she masturbated. Why couldn't I satisfy her in this way?

My boner dissolved in my hand as quickly as it came.

Maria rocked the entire bed as she began to ram herself with the dildo. She was no longer able to contain her moans. They echoed through the bedroom, taunting me.

A fucking piece of plastic was fucking my wife better than I ever could!

Her hips bucked as her fingers swirled around her swollen clit. She arched back and began to settle on my side of the bed.

I felt like I didn't belong there. Like I was an intruder. In my own bed. With my own wife.

As she frolicked, I saw the little wet spot on the sheets she left behind. My sad little wet spot. It looked pathetic. So did I.

I climbed off the bed and left the room. My wife's passionate cries continued without me. As if I had never been there.

About an hour later, she finally joined me in the kitchen. She was wearing a white robe. Her face had a glow that lit up the whole room. Her long blonde hair was unruly in an almost unruly way. She was stunning. As always.

But even as she leaned over and kissed me, I felt the anger building. But this time it was even more irrational. I thought about the dildo and realized that it had penetrated deeper into Maria than I ever would.

I was jealous of the dildo.

What the hell was wrong with me?

"What's wrong with me?" Maria's eyes were so innocent.

I hated myself for being mad at her. Why did she have to have sex with these other guys? Why couldn't she wait for me? Even though she didn't know me then, she had to know that I was somehow out there in her future.

"What's wrong with you?" she asked again. "Please talk to me."

I looked into her beautiful eyes as I felt tears welling up in my own eyes. I wanted to cry in front of her like a little sissy.

Her eyes turned to sadness that matched mine as she pulled my head to her chest in a hug.

Of course, I could never tell her the truth. It was so shameful that I would embarrass myself like this in front of her. But the present situation could not go on like this.

When she hugged me, I was able to avoid her eyes. And I was able to tell her what I was trying to do.

"You want other men to have sex with me?"

She no longer held me. She was alone on the couch, curled up in her robe, holding a pillow in front of her. Like a shield. To protect herself from me.

"No," I said, but it sounded hollow even to me.

"I want you to be my husband. Not my pimp!" Now she was crying.

I rushed to her side and held her hand. "No, sweetie, it's not like that at all."

She looked at me with watery eyes. "Then what is it like?"

Rarely did I have trouble explaining a concept. That's how I got so rich. But I had trouble explaining why I wanted my wife to sleep with other guys.

"I want you to feel good. Satisfied, I mean. During sex. I saw you in there and realized I couldn't give you that kind of pleasure."

"I don't care," she said, "I love you, and I thought you liked watching me."

"I do, too. I like it. I love watching you."

Mary sat in silence for about a minute while her sobs subsided. She looked like she was thinking about everything.

Finally, she reached out and grasped my hand in hers. "You are the only man I have ever loved," she said with her eyes locked on mine. "I love you and I trust you. And I want you to be happy. If you think that's something we should do, then I'm okay with that."

My heart felt like it was going to break. When she finished speaking, I had to hold her. She trembled at my touch, but she hugged me back. She put all her trust in me. I only wish I knew for sure that we were doing the right thing.

Later that night, we discussed some details. The ground rules, so to speak. First, she would choose who she slept with. In her mind, this reduced some of the "squeamish" features of the arrangement. Good. I had enough problems with women. I would probably be even worse at choosing men for sex.

Second, I would always be present at the... Encounter I would always be present. For the whole thing. From the first encounter to the.... Consummation.

That really bugged me. I was already having trouble dealing with their previous liaisons. How the hell was I supposed to react when such an encounter happened right in front of me?

Third, as far as sex was concerned, anything is possible. If Maria agreed to engage in an act in the heat of the moment, it was her prerogative.

Fourth, there would be no complaints from me. As far as Maria was concerned, the whole thing was my idea, and I had to deal with the consequences, "Like a man," she said. I felt this was ironic, since my inability to satisfy my wife like a man was part of the problem.

There were a number of other issues that we didn't address. This was obviously new territory for both of us. And we were uncomfortable asking others about our plan (Mary was unaware that my therapist had suggested this).

In every other facet of my life, I checked the data and reviewed my options before making a decision. And as a result, I had very few regrets. In this case, since I wasn't able to do it right, it scared me to death. I took a big risk and hoped I wouldn't regret it.

My apprehension grew as the first "encounter" approached. Mary took care of all the details. And she refused to tell me any of it. I had to give her credit for really knowing who she was married to.

But when she left our bedroom in a new, dark red cocktail dress that clung to her incredible body in all the right places, I almost called the whole thing off.

She twirled in front of me like we were going on our own date. Unfortunately, I was about to hand her over to a stranger who was lucky enough to see her. I wanted to rip her dress off and throw her on the bed. Let me enjoy her first and leave the sloppy seconds to the other guy.

The red ("Scarlett" according to Maria) dress was made of some fabric that was almost as smooth as Maria's skin. The dress highlighted her lack of a bra. And it didn't look like she had any panties on either.

We got into the car downstairs and the driver drove off, apparently already knowing about the destination. Even the driver knew more than I did. He was a tall, good-looking guy, and for a minute I had the thought that he was Maria's date(?).But he drove us to the Hilton hotel downtown and dropped us off.

Maria went ahead, and I followed her to the hotel bar off the main lobby. We sat at the end of the crowded bar. My eyes darted around the room, afraid that some guy there might be the one who was about to fuck my wife.

One problem with sitting at the end of the bar was that it was near the men's room. So for every guy that walked by us and stared or smiled at Maria, I imagined him sticking his cock in Maria. The images hurt me, but also made me hard. How messed up am I?

I caught our reflection in the mirror behind the bar. Maria was by far the most beautiful woman in there.Too bad she was sitting with a guy who looked like he had just been sentenced to death.

"Are you sure you want to do this?"

My eyes met Maria's and I wanted so badly to say no. But I couldn't, the status quo made me miserable. So I said, "Yes."

The rational part of my brain that was still functioning told me I wouldn't risk too much. She was already with three or six other guys. I imagined that each guy had a 20-cm dick - that's five feet from the dicks of the other guys in my wife. Five feet of dick. What's one more?

My self-pity and self-loathing shot up inside me as I became aware of his presence. It was strange. It was as if I sensed he was approaching.

He was the tallest guy in the room. He was easily six feet tall and dwarfed me. He had longer hair that looked unruly in a staged way. So did his unshaven face. He even wore jeans and a t-shirt that showed off his abs and whatever muscles were in his upper arms. And he was handsome, too, which fucking killed me. It was like he was answering a casting call from Hollywood for a ruggedly handsome bad boy.

It pissed me off watching him scan the room for my wife. He was a guy who could get any woman in the world. Why did he have to show up at mine?

Maria invited him!

Maria saw him, too. She looked past me to him and waved. She crossed her legs and uncrossed them. She was trembling just looking at him. I was sure she was wet with excitement, too.

"Hey," he said, walking toward my wife. "You must be Maria."

Maria remained seated. He and Maria both looked at me as I stood up and was only a few inches shorter than him. Then I stepped down from the rung of my bar stool. Like a damn fool, I looked up at him like a little kid looks up at his father.

Mary stood up and introduced herself, but not me. Just as well. He knew I was her husband. It was easy to tell by the mocking disdain he showed me. It was clear he had zero respect for me, a man who couldn't satisfy his own wife. And who would watch an expert do it for him.

They shook hands. His massive paw enveloped hers. I hoped there was no correlation between the size of his hand and the size of his cock.

His name was Peter. Maria asked him if he wanted a drink, but he said no. It felt so awkward, the three of us standing there, I was sure someone would just say they wanted to forget the whole thing. But no one did.

"So, are you ready?" asked Peter, as if he had something better to do.

Mary looked at me as she nodded. "I think so," she said. She pulled a hotel key card out of her purse. "Let's go upstairs."

They walked together like a couple. I followed them like an eerie third wheel. Even from behind, I saw other people looking at them as we passed the hotel lobby. They looked like they belonged together. I wanted to scream, "She's my wife! She's just going to fuck this guy, but I'm married to her!"

We entered a waiting elevator and were about to go up when an older man stopped closing the doors and entered with us. He excused himself while staring at Maria. He must have liked what he saw. The old pervert was obviously eye fucking her. That made me angry for a second. Then I remembered that I accompanied another guy upstairs to fuck her properly.

We got off on the fourteenth floor, which was really the unfortunate thirteenth floor, but no one would acknowledge it.

The room was nice, but I entered it with trepidation. In the middle of the room was a huge double bed. And in the far corner by the window was a chair where the pathetic husband sat watching another man use his wife as a fuck doll.

"So," Maria said. Her voice seemed a little shaky. But she was also excited. She grabbed my hand and pulled me toward her. "Last chance," she whispered.

She looked me in the eye, and I knew she wanted to do it. How could I tell her no after dragging her this far? My opportunity to say no was long gone.

I kissed her hard on the lips. My best performance. When it was done, I said, "Don't forget me."

"Of course not," she said. She gestured to the chair. "Watch me from there. And enjoy it."

She kissed me and escorted me to my seat. The show was about to begin.

Maria left me behind and walked over to Peter. She kissed him on the lips and let the straps of her dress slide off her shoulders. Then she tugged at the dress and her large, soft breasts stood out. She pulled his head to her chest and he began to kiss and caress her. As he did so, he licked and sucked her hard nipples, even though he had two huge greedy handfuls of them.

And already I was hard as a rock. Anger, desire and humiliation were buzzing around inside me. I was afraid he was hurting her by squeezing her tits so hard, but

Maria didn't seem to mind at all. Her eyes were closed and her head was thrown back, but her hands were around Peter's head, pulling him to her chest.

She stood back up and let her dress fall to her feet. She stood in front of him in her little red thong panties and black pumps. He leaned over and kissed her belly. She ran her hands through his thick, subdued hair. His huge hands soon found their way to my wife's smooth ass. He squeezed her ass and pulled her so far apart that I could see Maria's puckered asshole behind the thong.

His mouth moved down between her legs and kissed the panties covering her pussy. He hooked a finger on each side of her panties and pulled them down. The red panties hung a little between her thighs and she spread her legs a little wider to release them. This allowed him to slide his tongue against her cunt. He rubbed it with his hand and felt her wetness. She stepped out of the panties that had fallen to her ankles.

So there was Maria, my wife, completely naked with another man. His fingers and tongue ran wildly between her thighs, tasting her sweet juices.

He laughed as she pulled his white T-shirt over his head. Then her hands dropped to the bulge in his jeans. She stroked the outline of his hard cock in his pants. He seemed huge, and all I could think of was her huge dildo at home.

If his cock is as big as that damn thing, I'll jump out the goddamn window, I thought.

She continued to rub it through the fabric of his jeans. Then she kissed him again before turning her attention to unbuttoning his pants. He helped her by unbuttoning them. Then she unzipped his fly and pulled his pants down. His boxers tightened to contain his massive erection.

This was it, I thought. My last chance before his cock actually comes out and goes into her mouth. We can leave right now and just pretend this never happened. I can still stop this...

Maria pulled down his underwear and his huge cock sprang free. She dropped to her knees in front of him and bent down to kiss the side of his cock. She moved slowly. At first. Or maybe I was just seeing her in slow motion.

Then she put the head in her mouth and looked up at him. I collapsed in my seat, crushed. She was really doing it. She was really sucking another guy's cock.

Peter closed his eyes as her lips went all the way down his shaft. His long cock must have entered her throat, but she didn't gag. His huge hands were on her shoulders while her pretty blonde head bobbed up and down. Peter moaned and I saw Maria cupping his balls in her hand. And then she moved her mouth to them and sucked them too.

It hurt to watch my wife suck this man's cock. Even though I had a hard-on, I didn't like it at all. It was way too personal. His cock was in her face. The face I saw every day. And kissed every day. I should have at least banned blowjobs.

Suddenly Peter pushed her head away and helped Maria to her feet. Maria looked down and wiped the saliva from her lips.

Naked and without Maria wearing her pumps, he towered over her. His hard cock seemed almost as big as her forearm. I was suddenly afraid he was going to hurt her.

He lifted Maria with relative ease. For a moment I thought he was going to lower her onto his cock and fuck her while he stood in the middle of the room.

And then he began to do just that.

Maria spread her legs and wrapped them around him. He lowered her down onto his stiff cock. She was really wet and his cock slid easily into her. First halfway and then all the way down.

Wow, I thought. I was actually admiring how this giant was fucking my wife. My own cock was so hard doing this that I couldn't take it anymore. I unzipped my pants and pulled down my underwear and started stroking my own cock. As humiliating as it was to masturbate in the corner because another man was using my wife for his own pleasure, I had to do it.

He lifted her up and down. Maria whimpered as he penetrated her. Her head rested against his chest as every inch entered her.

Then he raised and lowered her one last time. She slid all the way down his shaft with her mouth open in a silent scream. Then he began to walk her to the bed. Mary's arms wrapped around his strong neck as he strode, and he gently lowered her back onto the bed.

My own cock throbbed as I watched him do something I could never do with Maria. I was so mortified that I must have been sobbing or something, because Peter was looking over at me, even though he was deep inside my wife.

He must have seen me, the pathetic wimp of a husband, jerking off in a chair not five feet from his wife and her lover. The sneer and derision on his face made fun of me. He would reach deeper into Mary than I ever would, and we both knew it.

After humiliating me with his gaze, he turned his attention back to my wife. Now that Maria was safely on her back on the bed, he pulled out his long cock. As he pulled it back, it seemed to go on and on forever. It reminded me of a sword swallower I had seen at a carnival when I was a kid. Only now the guy pulled his huge meat sword out of my wife.

Peter surprised me and Maria when he got down on his knees and put his face between her spread thighs. She cried out as his tongue entered her. She moaned and he pulled out. He began to lick and suck on her clit. He licked for a few seconds and then sucked her clit with his lips for a few more seconds. Maria's whole body twitched. He was like a puppeteer pulling her strings.

I knew she couldn't take much more. She held his head while her hips rocked. He reached up and pinched her erect nipples. She shook for about an hour, and I was pretty sure she was experiencing the biggest orgasm she'd ever had.

But he wasn't done with my wife yet.

He stood up and pushed his cock into her again. Mary was spent, but he rammed it into her again and again. Everything he had. As if he was determined to pound her right into the bed.

On and on he went, plunging into her again and again. Then, seemingly out of nowhere, he began to breathe heavily and his body began to shake. He was shaking and having trouble keeping his rhythm. I expected him to pull out and cover my wife with his cum.

But that didn't happen. Instead, he continued to pump into Maria. I felt numb as I watched this big man pump every drop of his semen deep inside Maria.

At this point, I could only assume that Peter was coming inside of Maria on Maria's instructions. I wasn't sure why that bothered me after everything else he had done to her. All I knew was that it just was.

When he was done fucking my wife, he pulled his long shaft out of her and made sure every drop of him stayed inside her.

He stepped away from the bed and stepped right in front of me. His massively swollen cock was still hard and was right at my eye level. I don't know why he was standing there like that, other than to humiliate me even further. His cock glistened with my wife's juices covering every inch.

He grinned at me as if challenging me to do something about it. All I could do was look away in shame.

Peter got dressed and left without a word, leaving me and Maria to clean up the mess.

Maria was still lying naked on the bed. She hadn't moved since Peter had pulled out of her. If she hadn't been breathing, I would have thought he had killed her there.

Seeing her there and thinking about what Peter had just done to her made me so uncomfortable. I looked down at Maria's normally pretty pussy. Her perfect porcelain skin had red marks where Peter had been too forceful, especially on her breasts and inner thighs. But it was her cunt that caught my attention the most.

Her cunt was still gaping open from Peter's massive shaft. It looked like it extended far beyond anything she had before. A steady stream of Peter's cum was also oozing out of her.

It was disgusting. Disgusting. But something inside me kept churning. It was exciting me, and I had no idea why.

I climbed into position between Maria's spread legs. The scent of sex and sweaty bodies seemed strangely out of place. Unnatural to me. These smells were usually present after my participation, not before.

I rubbed the tip of my cock against Maria's dripping cunt. I tried to push away the thought that another man's cum was dripping from my wife, but I couldn't. This made me even hotter.

I plunged my cock into her gaping hole. She felt so lost to me. The tight channel I had come to know had been stretched far beyond anything I could do. But it still felt great.

I thrust in and out of Maria as fast as I could. Her breasts rocked wildly back and forth. But she wasn't even looking at me. Her face was fixed on the ceiling. And perhaps her eyes were closed.

All too soon, I felt my release approaching. I tried to delay it, but couldn't. I started pumping my load into her.

Normally, I would have collapsed in her arms. But this time I didn't. When I was done, she paid no attention to me. No, "Are you okay?" Or, "How was that?"

Panic filled me. She was unconscious! The thought that Peter's rough fucking had actually killed her scared me more than anything I had ever experienced.

I pulled out of her and crawled onto her side. I pressed my fingers to her throat and felt for a pulse. She was alive. I sighed in relief.

Her eyes fluttered open, and I realized what had happened. She had fallen asleep. While I was fucking her!

"Hey," she said. She blinked and looked around. Then she must have realized what had happened. "I'm sorry."

"It's okay," I said. But it wasn't. Not even close.

She sat up slowly. "Uh. I'm so sore," she said.

I rolled my eyes behind her back.

She stood up, shaky on her feet. "I have to go to the bathroom." Her steps looked awkward. Either she was really sore or there were just two loads of cum dripping out of her and didn't want it dripping down her thighs. Probably a little of both.

As she closed the bathroom door, I stared at the bed. Just below where her butt lay on the bed was a huge glob of cum. The sight of it humiliated me. My cum and another guy's cum mixed together. And it was dripping from my wife's cunt.

With a handful of tissues, I tried to wipe it up. The sticky liquid stuck to my fingers and I shivered. It was so disgusting that I wanted to chop off my hand rather than wash it.

The shower was on when I opened the bathroom door. Behind the transparent glass, I could see the indistinct figure of my wife. I scrubbed my hand in the sink with a new bar of soap and boiling hot water.

"Hey," Maria called out. "Get in here."

As I looked at my reflection in the quickly fogging mirror, I tried to suppress the bad feelings. Letting another man fuck my wife while I watched, and cleaning up his cum after he was done with her, was the most humiliating thing that had ever happened to me. I was pathetic.

Maria stuck her head out. She had a big smile on her face and beckoned me over to her. Her wet arms encircled me and pulled me into her warm, wet, naked body.

She pulled me under the hot water and kissed me. "I love you, you know." She took a bar of soap and began to lather my body. "And I hope you got what you wanted out of it."

Her hands roamed over my cock and balls. Her soapy fingers massaged all around, and I got hard again. "And if nothing else, know that I would do anything for you."

In that moment, alone with my beautiful, loving wife in the shower, I finally felt better. Lighter. A weight had been lifted from my shoulders. All the humiliation was gone, at least temporarily. I knew it would come back eventually, but I was happy. For the moment.

WITH HIS BOSS

Restlessly, I check the oven temperature for the fifth time before turning the spoon through the sauce simmering on the stove for the hundredth time. Everything has to be perfect tonight.

"Remember, honey, everything has to be perfect tonight." It's like she's inside my head, reading my mind.

"Yes, honey." I turn and smile at her, my lovely, gorgeous wife. She's wearing an incredible looking slinky black dress that I've never seen before. Steak is not the only thing on the menu tonight.

" Darling." Her voice is firm and shakes me out of my thoughts.

"Hmm?"

"The sauce, dear, don't forget to stir it.

I blush, "Yes, dear."

She's right, tonight has to be perfect. Tonight, at my own invitation, my boss is coming to our home for dinner. Mr. Gramms; Christian Gramms.

I invited him because I know I'm in for a big promotion, and I'm not ashamed to dip my toes in a little ass kissing as I get on with my nag.

But there is another reason Mr. Gramms is coming tonight.

He has made his intentions clear several times, even before I had to admit to myself that I was incapable of taking care of my wife the way she needed to be treated. Yes, he had his eye on her long before I admitted that I was less of a man than I thought I was at that point in my life; a bald head, a fat belly, and an 8-cm dick that barely did anything for Katrin.

I know they say it's not the size, it's how you use it, but usually there are limits. Cheap wine will still taste like shit no matter how much soda water and ice cubes you dump into it.

So yes, Mr. Gramms had made his thoughts about my wonderful, pretty, young wife pretty clear before the invitation. At the office party last year, I had watched him place his hands on her back as he laughed at a joke of hers before so subtly dropping it on her perfect butt. He had let his hand linger there, just resting on the soft, curved swell of her ass, and he had turned and winked at me, watching the color drain from my face before he removed it completely. Katrin didn't know I'd even seen it, and she'd never mentioned it.

But I had seen it; I had seen my wife blush at his touch, and in a flirty, eager way that was not unpleasant.

Quick comments had become darker and more meaningful in the workplace. "Hey Schmidt, how's your wife?" had morphed dramatically into "How's your sexy little wife?" and "A guy like you better hold on to that Katrin, Schmidt; someone might come and take her away from you" in a very short time.

After that, she came by the office more and more often, dressing better and sexier each time. It finally got to a point where I wasn't even trying to pretend she wasn't there for me anymore as she breezed past my desk to his office.

And that's when I knew that if this marriage was going to last, I had to admit that this was my fault. I had to swallow my masculine dignity and accept that my pathetic excuse for a dick and my desperate and terrible attempts to make love were failing the beautiful, sexually prime woman whose basic needs I had to satisfy.

That's also when I realized I could kill two birds with one stone, if you'll pardon the pun.

When I invited Mr. Gramms to dinner, his first question was, of course, "And will your lovely wife be joining us?"

After that, I think I actually always knew that it was inevitable to eventually end up here, where we are now.

He had started by always coming to the men's room while I was there. He casually sidled up to the urinal next to mine and unzipped it before letting his cock fall violently out of his pants. The guy was fucking huge, and he knew it.

He also knew I was sneaking peeks at him every time. He never said anything, but his smug looks and further inquiries about my wife as we both stood there with our hilariously unequal dicks told me everything.

So when I knew what to do - when I finally admitted to my wife and myself that I wasn't man enough to satisfy her, I knew that the answer to both of our problems lay with him. Hell, if I let my wife sleep with another man, it might help me advance my career, too.

I expected her to protest first; to fight me, to bring up the sanctity of our vows, to mock me for trying to sell her to my boss for a promotion within the company, even if that wasn't what it was. But to my shock, and almost horror, she had readily agreed to the plan.

" Wait," I stammered after the lengthy conversation in which I laid out my own inadequacies and how I

thought it would be good for both of us to allow her
what she needed;

"That's it, just like that it's a yes?"

She cocked her head and looked at me deadpan; "That's
it of course honey". She licked her lips, a fiery excited
look in her eyes that I hadn't seen in a very long time.

"If you're asking if I want this, the answer is yes".

I had swallowed hard; I had embarked on the long and
frustrating journey of being a cuckold, and my wife was
in the driver's seat.

After that, I couldn't even pretend it was about me. In a
way, it helped me because I no longer felt guilty for
feeling like I was "selling out" my wife to advance my
own career. No, it was about her now; she made that
very clear. Any benefits that came my way were purely
secondary.

I hadn't said anything openly to Mr. Gramms, but he knew. I had knocked on his office door and entered his spacious office with a pang of jealousy; the huge shelves lined with books, the amazing view of the city, the huge oak desk with the expensive silver knickknacks that only rich people keep on their desks.

He had asked me to take off my shoes with a small, smug grin on his face. Yes, he knew why I was here, and he wanted to make me even smaller while I asked. A big bull stallion like Mr. Gramms knew a little cuckold when he saw one.

I had walked across the carpeted office to his desk in my socks; he didn't ask me to sit down. I invited him to dinner and said that we, "my wife and I," would be happy to have him over. If he wasn't sure beforehand, the way my face reddened, the way my tongue felt heavier in my throat, told him everything he needed to know. The "dinner" was bullshit, a guy like Christian Gramms knew that, and a guy like him could also see that I was here, submissively approaching his throne in my socks, begging him to fuck my wife.

"So this has nothing to do with the promotion speculation going around the office?". He laughed at

me, daring me to admit that this was a way for me to
pay my way into office.

I stumbled and stuttered in my way as a beta about my
choice of words. No, I assured him, that wasn't even the
point! We just wanted the pleasure of his company at
our home.

"We, huh?" Mr. Gramms stared at me across the desk,
his eyes twinkling, almost as if he were considering the
offer. He finally stood up, his tall, imposing physique
filling out his expensive suit, making me look jealous.

"All right, it's a deal, Schmidt."

And that brings us to tonight; tonight when everything
had to be perfect.

Katrin looked fucking fantastic. She was wearing a
form-fitting, tight and short black dress with a plunging
neckline. I looked at her desperately and jealously,
cursing my jeans for denying me the ability to even
remotely satisfy this woman who had confusingly agreed
to spend her life with me.

If that was what it took to make her happy, to keep her with me, then so be it.

*****

"The roast is excellent, Katrin."

My wife blushes flirtatiously in front of Mr. Gramms and takes a sip of her wine as she bends shyly toward him. God, she's acting like a little schoolgirl with a crush.

"Oh, actually, Hans has been cooking." Herr. Gramms just smirks as he takes another bite.

"Of course he cooked." He looks at me across the table and winks. I swallow hard.

"Schmidt;" he keeps calling me by my last name, as if we're still in the office and he's still my supervisor. This annoys me somehow.

"Would you mind giving me some more of that delicious sauce?". He looks at me sharply, with a grinning expression on his face. Katrin is almost hanging on his arm, completely ignoring me as she gazes at his perfect jawline. Her eyes wander over his chest, a line of muscle definition showing at the top of his shirt where the buttons have been left undone.

He wants me out of the room, I know it.

"Absolutely!" I say it way too eagerly and leave my seat with a groveling grin on my face. "I'll just, ah, go...ah, get the sauce."

Mr. Gramms just looked at me and smiled thinly.

In the kitchen, I try to catch my breath, try to slow the pounding pulse in my chest.

Holy crap, this is really happening! That's him getting the reigns on me in front of Katrin. Should the man go get him food from the kitchen? Yeah, none of us will have any illusions about what the dynamics are here and now after this. Just as no one here will have any illusions about why he's really here for dinner.

I stand over the sink and splash cold water on my face. Am I ready for this? Am I really ready to accept my place as a wimp and let my boss fuck my beautiful wife?

I breathe and count to ten. I take a deep breath, turn around and head back to the dining room.

I am just shying away from the door back into the room when I realize I haven't even brought the sauce yet! I curse under my breath and turn around when I hear it.

"Oh, very good baby, this mouth feels amazing.

I freeze and almost collapse in the hall as my bowels fall out from underneath.

Son of a bitch! Is he doing it NOW? Is he really going to fuck my wife right there in my dining room while we're having fucking dinner?

I'm sweating now, chilled; am I ready for this? I take a deep breath, steel myself, and stride around the corner and into the room.

My world is crumbling beneath me.

Mr. Gramms is standing next to my wife's chair, one hand on his hip and the other holding her hair. But what really catches my eye is the fact that her lips - my wife's fucking lips - are wrapped tightly around my boss's huge, throbbing cock.

If I thought it was big before, when I see it soft when I pee, it's absolutely massive while it's hard and dripping my wife's spit. As she slowly slides her lips off his flaring cockhead, I actually gasp at his size. He is easily three, maybe four times my length; the shaft is strong and muscular. Katrin's hand is wrapped around it, but her fingers are unable to grip all the way around its fat circumference. I imagine the two of us standing side by side, cocks stretched out and hard, and the comparison is almost ridiculous.

His pants are down over his muscular and toned thighs around his knees, and he holds her hair tightly as she bobs her lips up and down his shaft. Her eyes are wide open, staring into his face with a look of absolute lust and servitude; of worship of the Lord with the huge cock filling her mouth.

Her hands caress his shaft, which is so long it won't fit in her mouth, and her fingers play with his heavy hanging balls as she loudly bobs and sucks on his thick girth. She hasn't even glanced at me as I enter the room, but Mr. Gramms raises his eyes to me.

"Ah, Schmidt!" He says it as if addressing a co-worker late to the bar after work. His eyes fall on my empty hands and he frowns.

"Schmidt, you forgot the sauce."

I feel leaden, glued to the spot. This man is getting a blowjob, from MY WIFE, in my house, in my living room, in front of me! And here he is asking me about fucking gravy?

I'm not even sure he's serious until he repeats himself.

"Schmidt, the gravy. If you please."

His eyes bore into mine, the only sound in the room my own heartbeat pounding in my ears and the loud, moaning, groaning, sucking sounds of my wife's mouth on his cock. Silently, obediently, I turn around, feeling shame and humiliation, and make my way back to the kitchen.

"And a scotch would be wonderful, Schmidt," he calls after me.

I return to the living room even more humiliated, feeling more like his servant by the minute, to find my wife's mouth still against Herr Gramss impressive flesh; now that the straps of her dress are sliding down her arms and one, perfect, full and round breast slipped out and lay exposed. Mr. Gramms plays with her erect and bright pink nipple as she sucks obediently and wantonly.

He turns around and just smiles at me, in the same smug way he does when he asks me to stay late on a Friday or

fill in for another employee when he takes this man out
for golf or lunch.

I know I should be angry, offended even. But really, he
has every right to look at me that way. Here's a man
who really is better than me; he's successful, wealthy,
handsome, and he has a dick that puts mine to shame.
And on top of that, I can't even say, "Well, I have
Katrin," because there she is now, with her lips happily
wrapped around HIS cock!

"Schmidt, would you bring the scotch?" He stares at me.
"You can skip the sauce, I think I'm done with dinner.

Is he serious? I stand rooted to the spot, feeling like a
servant getting the master his drink. What am I, a
bartender?

"Schmidt." His voice is commanding and sharp, and his
hard gaze makes my eyes quickly rise from his glistening,
throbbing cock, which disappears in and out of my
wife's pouty lips and reaches up to his face.

"Bring it here."

I swallow and slowly put one foot in front of the other.
Hesitantly, haltingly, eyes wide with a mixture of
jealousy and humiliation, but also with a hint of
something exciting, I bring my boss his scotch while my
wife gives him a blowjob.

He takes it from my slightly trembling, submissive hands
and smiles warmly at me, as if his gratitude were a gift I
would appreciate. He sips the scotch, then hands it back
to me.

"Would you do me a favor, Schmidt? Why don't you
take this upstairs to the bedroom; we'll be right up."

My God, he is so blunt, so blatantly clear that he is
going to fuck my wife tonight. His eyes close, and he
seems to sense the hum in my demeanor.

"Now Schmidt, don't be like that." His words are
interrupted by the slurping sound emanating from my
wife's mouth as she sucked his cock into her warm
mouth.

"We both know why I'm here. He pulls his cock out of Katrin's lips with a wet pop as she looks up at him lovingly and lustfully. Gently, he taps the heavy girth of his shaft against her cheek and then pushes the head over her big red lips.

"If you had that, you wouldn't be in this position and wouldn't need me here to satisfy this gorgeous woman," he says. Katrin smiles at him and blushes at his flattery while completely ignoring me.

He's right, and I know it. I nod and take the glass from him.

" Good boy, Schmidt," he calls after me as I humbly slink out of the room.

Upstairs, I place his scotch on my nightstand and pace the room as I feel my blood freeze in my veins and my stomach twist inside me. I know it's too late to back out, but a million thoughts race through my head. Am I really ready to trade my wife for a promotion?

I also realize I'm worrying about what to do up here;
now and when they come. Does he want me to stay?
Should I leave? For some reason, I find myself in bed
on my usual side over the covers. My clothes stay on,
but I decide, oddly enough, that taking off my shirt will
loosen me up.

There I am, still sitting, ten minutes later, when they
enter the room. Katrin giggles and wipes her mouth as
she holds Mr. Gramms by the hand and leads his tail,
bobbing heavily in front of him, into our bedroom.

She looks at me pointedly, her eyes glowing, a hungry
desire clearly painted across her face, and the way her
reddened chest heaves with each breath.

"Where do you want me?" She looks me in the eye, but
she asks him.

"Why don't you crawl into bed with your husband,
honey? He smiles at me. "I want you right there on the
bed, face down."

She giggles and willingly crawls onto the bed next to me. Our eyes meet, and where mine show concern, alarm, and need for reassurance, hers show only boldness, hunger, and an erotic charge that almost scares me.

Katrin lies face down next to me in bed, where we lie every night, even though there is no routine in our current version of the scenario. Mr. Gramms kneels on the bed behind her and moves between her legs.

"Let's just get that perfect ass up there, Katrin." He murmurs to my wife, who eagerly sucks in her bottom lip and lifts her hips off the bed.

Behind her, my boss slowly strokes his enormous length as his eyes sink into my wife's perfect ass. I know this view, I've been there. My stomach churns as I wonder if I'll ever be allowed that view again after she gets a taste of a real man.

Mr. Gramms straightens his cock and presses it against my wife. A slight moan escapes her lips, and I see her eyelids flutter as his massive cockhead begins to press between her lips. He begins to thrust forward, sliding his enormous girth into my wife. She moans erotically as his enormous girth stretches her pussy wide as he slowly impales her with his big thick cock.

He's no more than an inch or two in before he pauses and starts shaking his head as he looks at me.

"So Schmidt, I know I asked, but are you sure this has nothing to do with all the talk of promotion floating around the office?

I shake my head meekly side to side and stammer.

"N-no, Mr. Gramms, nothing like that."

He nods and arches his eyebrows thoughtfully as Katrin impatiently begins to push his cock back. He lets a few more inches of his magnificent cock slide into her before his hands stop her and halt his thrusting.

"That's very good to hear, Schmidt." He arches his forehead at me. His mouth opens as if to say something, but then he shakes his head again with a giggle. And with that, he thrusts forward mightily and buries the rest of his cock deep inside my wife.

Katrin grunts with the force of his thrust, and then her mouth goes slack in a low, exquisite-looking whine of pleasure.

Mr. Gramms pulls back, grips her hips powerfully in his grip, and buries the rest of his cock 25 cms deep inside her with ease. Beside me, my wife moans, her face scrunched up in a look that can only be described as pure pleasure as my boss's big cock slides through her wet folds. Her hands clutch the sheets, her knuckles white as she pleasurably turns over our sheets.

I stare at this beautiful woman and realize that I was just holding her back. This is how you have to take a beautiful, sensual creature like Katrin; hard, deep and with a massive boner from a man.

And with that, my boss starts fucking her with a deep, powerful rhythm. She jerks forward with each thrust, gasping and moaning in pleasure, and I can hear the wet sounds of her cunt opening up for him. I can literally hear how turned on she is as she is taken by this alpha stud's big cock, and I just want to hide. But at the same time, I can't tear my eyes away.

"Tell me Katrin, did you date anyone before you became Mrs. Schmidt?

Oh God, he's going to go there. Of course, I'm not the first man Katrin dated, but her dating history was, well, let's just say, sometimes a point of contention between us. My wife is a caring, amazing woman, but when we first started dating, it took a lot for me to get over her bad girl past; probably because of my own insecurities.

Mercifully, I don't know the whole story, but I do know that she was a bit wild in college and certainly had a raunchy reputation with the football team. Again, it was always something I never wanted to bring up, and she was only ever willing to do the same. But now here we are, and I know she's going to tell him all the things I never wanted to hear.

As if my humiliation wasn't complete enough, having my boss fuck my own wife in my own bed while I watch it happen; he's also going to make her tell him what a slut she was.

"No...I...I had before...ugh....." Each of her words is interrupted by a hard thrust from Mr. Gramm's thick cock, which plunges into her pussy. His balls slapping loudly against her as he plunges into her cunt.

"Those other men; were they bigger than your husband?".

Oh for fuck's sake. I want to curl up and sink through the floor. Of course they were bigger than me! He saw me in the men's room at work, hell, he knows why he's here. But he wants to hear her say it; he wants to hear my cuckolded humiliation become complete.

"Oh God, yes!" Katrin's eyes open wide, and she rolls them back in her head as he grips her hips and slaps her pussy with his big thick cock.

"Much bigger?" He turns to me and winks, not even breaking his rhythm as his muscular torso thrusts back and forth, sawing its girth in and out of my wife.

"My ex - before Hans - was pretty big! Ugh... Not as big as you, but big!" Her tits swing beneath her as he fucks her, her whole body jerking forward with each thrust and her mouth going slack with horniness. She never told me about the ex, mostly because I never wanted to hear it. But in our current situation, I'm suddenly terribly curious and at the same time terrified of what she's about to say.

"And what did he like to say?"

"He used to...oh god....he used to stick it up my butt!".

Shock washes over my face; her butt!? I stare at my wife in shock; who is this woman? I've asked before, of course I have, what man doesn't? But she has always, always turned me down. Maybe the ex dissuaded her?

"And did you enjoy shoving his big cock up your tight little ass?".

Now she's grunting and moaning, her hands gripping the sheets and her eyes squeezing shut. I know, just because I know her, that she's close.

Mr. Gramms seems to be able to tell, too. Part of me wants to be angry; outraged that this man who has met my wife three times seems to know her body as well as I do, someone who has been married to her for almost ten years. But then again, a man like him would know a woman like my wife well, and again, I have to admit my own shortcomings here.

Knowing that she is close to him, he seems to ease up and slow down his urges; he wants to tear it out of her, he wants to hear her humiliate me.

"Katrin? Did you do it?"

"Yes!" she practically screams it, the slutty and erotic moans pouring from her lips.

I stare at my wife, just stare at her, and she's getting fucked right next to me on our marital bed. I ask, I pester her for her ass, for years! And each time, I've been rebuffed. This is just another stage in the completion of my cuckoldry.

Mr. Gramms grins as he pulls out of my wife's cunt with an audible sucking sound. She gasps at the sudden emptiness.

"Schmidt;" my eyes twitch up to his. He looks at me smugly.

"You seem to be over there.... Left alone. Would you like to attend?"

I feel my pulse racing; he wants me to participate? For a moment, I feel blood rush to my tiny cock, and I almost instantly get a painful hard-on. I nod eagerly.

"Why don't you come back here?

I eagerly begin to pull on my belt buckle, but he stops me with a persistent motion of his hand.

"No, no, Schmidt. You can leave those on."

I look at him questioningly, obviously missing his meaning.

"I meant, why don't you come back here with your mouth on?

I stare at him, he stares back involuntarily, the faintest hint of a smirk on his face.

"Now, Schmidt."

His energetic direction jolts me awake, and I get up and shuffle down the bed. Mr. Gramms barely moves out of the way as I move my head close to my wife's gaping and red pussy, her lips swollen from fucking. My boss's cock bobs menacingly close to my head, and I swallow hard.

"Get in there, Schmidt. If you can't use that pathetic little excuse of a cock to satisfy your wife, then you damn well better be able to please her with your mouth."

I nod wholeheartedly. The man is right. Uncomfortably, I move forward and run my tongue over her gaping slit.

Immediately I make a face; I can clearly taste something new, something different in her. I blanch as I realize it's the taste of his pre-cum, his own musk, rubbed off on her like a calling card. He chuckles beside me as my realization obviously appears on my face.

"Yeah, get in there Schmidt, you keep the lady waiting here".

Katrin pushes back impatiently at my mouth, and I know he has left her close. She wants me to lick her; my wife wants me to taste her sex mixed with the scent of another man's cock after he fucks her.

I almost give up on the spot; I almost walk away from the whole thing.But the feeling that Katrin needs me, for the first time in, well, a very long time, convinces me that it's worth it; even if it means tasting my boss's pre-cum from her pussy. I take a deep breath and move in.

All I hear is laughter; conceited, smug laughter, from both of them! Mr. Gramms just chuckles, knowing how humiliated I feel, yet desperate to gain an ounce of their affection so I do.

I lick her for a few minutes, but I realize I'm getting nowhere. Despite my lack of cock and my terrible attempt to have sex, I haven't even bothered to get better at oral sex. Immediately, I am overcome with how little I have invested in this marriage as a man.

Finally, mercifully, he stops me.

"Okay, okay, I think you're done, Schmidt."

I sigh, ashamed, and start to back away.

"Not so fast." His voice stops me cold.

"I said you're done. Try higher."

Then what?

I turn and look at him as he strokes his big cock and looks at me smugly.

"Higher, Schmidt."

He rolls his eyes at my confused look and finally just reaches out and points.

"Here."

I concentrate and stand still; his finger rests on my wife's clenched and puckered asshole.

"Right here, Schmidt. I want you to give it a good lick and make it nice and wet for me."

I freeze and slowly try to comprehend what he is saying. I hear Katrin gasp and slowly turn to look at him. He just nods at me and grins.

" Nice and wet for me Schmidt. I need that asshole nice and wet for my cock".

My God, he wants me to polish my wife's ass to soap it up for him?

I feel like a slave; a worthless, humiliated slave. But here we are, at this point, and it's a feeling I've almost gotten used to. I bend over and lick.

It's humiliating, though part of it is exciting, because I know Katrin would never let me do this alone, not without her new bull telling her to do it.

But here and now, with her new stud, her bull watching and stroking his fat cock while I cream my own wife's ass for him, she loves it. She loves it so much that she willingly opens her mouth wide and lets him slide his still sticky and wet cock from her own cunt right past her lips and into her mouth.

Once again, something she would never have done with me.

I start more and more probing her ass with my tongue and heaping on the spit as I roll my tongue around and inside her clenched ass. If I can't actively fuck her ass, at least I can make sure she enjoys the experience. I want to hit myself right now for even thinking it. My God, I'm such a lousy bitch.

Mr. Gramms seems sufficiently impressed by my furtive and tentative licking, my drooling. Suddenly he is beside me again and pushes me away.

"Back to your seat, Schmidt."

And then he deftly pushes against her tight sphincter, pressing the huge knob of his cock against her asshole as he leans forward. Katrin gasps and moans, in total ecstasy right next to me as he does this. You can tell by the look on her face that she loves this; that this is something she had to do without while we were together. The shame that I withheld this from her, that I denied her this pleasure, burns within me.

When her eyes fly open and a deep, guttural moan escapes her lips, I know he's pushed his head past her tight ring. I exhale slowly, not even realizing I've been holding my own breath as I watch him slowly push the head in.

He slides forward, slippery on my spit. And then he fucks her tight, buttery ass with deep, steady, plowing motions, burying himself completely with each movement. His balls come to rest on her dripping pussy lips, and Katrin screams in orgasmic little mewling sounds that she's never made in my presence when he does that.

I know I deserve this; I know we're in this extremely humiliating situation here because I'm wearing fucking jeans and I'm a fucking husband. And lest we forget, because I agreed, no, I offered my wife in exchange for a chance at a promotion.

But, thank God, if for nothing else. I'm still not sure it's worth it to watch my beautiful wife get fucked in the ass by my boss's huge cock in hopes of a promotion at the end, but it at least keeps me sane while this is happening right next to me.

Katrin is really getting into it now, and she's pushing hard on his cock.

"Oh, fuck yeah! Fuck that slutty married ass Christian! Take my ass! Take it up the ass with your big fat cock! Use it! Take me whenever you want! My ass is yours and yours alone!"

My jaw drops at the filth pouring from the mouths of my wife, my significant other and my partner! I'm shocked and still totally humiliated, but at the same time I'm totally aroused! My little cock is rock hard in my pants! I long to touch it, to pull down my pants and just jerk it, even if only for a minute. But I know that's overkill; that's the humiliation I can't stand: jerking off and watching my wife get fucked in the ass. That's just too much.

Mr. Gramms begins pounding Katrin's ass with wild, pounding strokes. His balls slap and bounce violently off her pussy, her breasts bouncing wildly beneath her. And suddenly she comes, hard.

She shrieks and her eyes roll back in her head as her climax tears through her. In the ten fucking years I've been married, I've never, and I mean fucking never, even remotely seen anything like this from my wife.

She thrashes under his anal assault, and I can actually see clear liquid dripping copiously from her pussy and running down her legs to soak the sheets beneath. My god, he's making her cum with it!

Slowly he winds his deep thrust down Katrin's ass as she slowly comes down. And then he pulls out, turns her over and strokes himself.

"Schmidt, I think you should probably watch this next bit". He says this with a smirk. He moves to the bed on the other side of my wife, stroking his throbbing and huge cock. It's red and slippery and looks wet from her ass, and he moves close to her head.

Oh sweet Jesus, she's not really going to....

Oh, but she does. Without missing a beat, my sweet, beautiful wife opens her lips, juts her head up and sucks my boss's cock, right out of her ass and into her mouth!

My eyes almost pop out of my head as she moans like a total slut and takes his cock right out of her slutty little ass and into her mouth. Mr. Gramms throws his head back and moans loudly as she gags on his cock.

Suddenly he looks right at me and stabs me in the eye with his hard stare. I realize he's close, that my boss is about to cum in my wife's mouth.

"Oh, and Schmidt?" He grinds his jaw as he looks at me smugly.

"There's no promotion, I'm not sure who started the rumor".

My vision blackens at the corners, and just as the floor begins to fall away from under me, I suddenly see Katrin's lips and throat begin to suck vigorously as I hear Christian Gramms grunt loudly.

My boss comes, right into my wife's mouth.

With a scream, he pulls his throbbing cock from her hungry lips and starts fisting the thick, long cock. Huge white spurts of cum spurt from his flaring red cockhead and come of their own accord onto Katrin's upturned face. Pumping on and on, more cum shoots out of his throbbing cock and splashes down, covering my wife's face. She moans, her fingers buried in her pussy as his cum lands in thick streaks on her nose and forehead, covering her lips and cheeks and splattering over her outstretched and needy tongue.

And just like that, my cuckold humiliation is complete.

*****

I slept on the couch downstairs that night after Mr. Gramms kicked me out of the bedroom.

"I've been drinking, Schmidt, I'm not going to drive! That's no way to let a guest out of the house!" That's what he says to me in the doorway of Katrin and I's bedroom before slamming the door in my face. Downstairs, I masturbate quietly and furiously, and I fall asleep to the sound of my wife's cries of pleasure while my boss fucks her senseless until the wee hours of the morning.

*****

I'm groggy at work on Monday morning because Katrin has denied me access to my own bedroom since dinner with Mr. Gramms. In fact, she didn't talk to me much the rest of the weekend after that evening, except to point out a few chores around the house that I need to do and when I should start dinner.

The intercom on my phone flashes, and I answer it hastily.

"Yes?"

"Well, Schmidt, let's hear a little more pep in your voice!". It's Mr. Gramms.

"Schmidt, your wife has just arrived in my office". I feel a cold, excited chill grip my stomach. I hear Mr. Gramms groan a little on the phone and then chuckle.

"Why don't you come watch? Oh and Schmidt," he pauses, and I can practically hear the grin through the phone.

"Bring your tongue, we're going to need it."

CUCKOLD MADNESS

One of the reasons I became a college professor was my love for the energy and excitement that young people have. Heck, I loved it so much that I married one of my former students.

Two years ago, we got married. Janine was twenty-four, sixteen years younger than me. She was a former athlete and very athletic. Her body was toned and perfect, and I could hardly keep up with her.

Sometimes, however, I could not keep up with her at all.

It had been a relatively long time since we had been intimate. As with most couples, we started out hot and heavy, and over time things had gradually calmed down. But lately things had become extremely quiet, almost non-existent, and I couldn't even remember the last time we had sex.

All winter it seemed like the most exciting thing we did was go to the varsity soccer games. Fortunately, the team was very good and made it to the big end-of-season tournament in March. Madness, they called it.

It was fun to watch soccer and everyone except Janine was excited. She knew every player by name. For months, I just assumed she was going through her varsity athlete days while we watched. But then something happened after a close game.

It was a bitterly cold night, and a blizzard was expected to dump over a foot of snow on campus overnight. Lectures were already canceled for the next day, and the air in the arena was really exciting.

When our team finally won the game in overtime, many of the students rushed onto the court to celebrate. I figured Janine would like to stick around for a while and soak it all in. But I was way off base.

She wanted to leave right away.

So Janine pulled me by the hand up the stairs through the crowd and out into the cold night air. We practically ran home as the snow flurries fell from the sky around us.

My lungs screamed for air as we reached the front steps of our townhouse. With my hands on my knees, I gasped for air. "What are we doing here?"

Janine grabbed my hand and dragged me up the stairs, "I want you to ravage me."

Ravage?

I was good at a lot of things. But "ravaging" someone was not one of them.

Suddenly we were in our bedroom, and Janine quickly undressed. Underneath, she was wearing sexy lingerie. That told me that she had planned this all along.

Suddenly Janine bit her lower lip and eyed me like a wild animal ready to eat. She pounced on me and threw me on the bed. She started tearing at my jacket and tie, and then she ripped off my pants. My good pants!

It was pretty clear to me that she was excited, and I was too. I wasn't getting hard.

Janine frowned as she pulled down my boxers. My flaccid little cock was obviously not what she had expected. She started pulling and tugging on it, but it seemed to lie lifeless between her fingers. Almost as if he had passed out.

Janine shook her head as if she couldn't understand what the problem was. She seemed confused. How could this have happened?

I closed my eyes and tried to stiffen, but it was useless.

Janine sighed and seemed to regroup. She stroked me furiously, but there wasn't much for her to hold onto. My whole cock disappeared in her grip.

I was so embarrassed. I had long accepted the fact that I was not well endowed. But this particular problem had never come up before. So not only did I have a tiny cock, but I couldn't even get it up when my beautiful young athlete wife played with it.

As a last ditch effort, Janine pulled my flaccidity into her mouth and sucked. I looked down and watched as her lips slid over my soft member. The warm wetness of her mouth felt so good. She even played with my balls.

But even that didn't work. It only ever got half hard.

"I'm really sorry, baby," I said. "It must be the stress from work," I said. Or the cold."

Janine finally gave up and laid her head on my chest. Her disappointment was obvious. What was she supposed to feel? Her own husband didn't seem to have much desire for her.

How long had it really been since we last had sex? I just stared at the ceiling in the dark, wondering what we should do next.

"Are you still attracted to me?" asked Janine.

"Of course I am, honey. Why do you ask me that?" I stroked her long, silky hair.

"Because it's been so long since we've had sex."

"Has it been that long?"

"Yes, it's been that long."

"I guess you're right. It has been that long." My mind raced for a solution, but I couldn't think of anything. "What should we do?"

As it happened, Janine had a suggestion of her own. It shocked me when she first mentioned it. I was so angry and upset that I couldn't even talk about it for almost a week. During that time, I avoided Janine at every opportunity. It was lonely, but it gave me time to think about things. To think about what I really wanted.

And then I realized what I really wanted.

What I wanted most in the world was to make my wife, who I love more than anything, happy. That made things pretty simple.

As I walked around our living room in front of the couch and the large picture window, I felt nauseous. I coughed several times. It was those deep coughing fits you get right before you throw up. Twice I even had to run to the bathroom because I thought I was really going to throw up. But nothing came. Just dry heaves. From my nerves.

This was such a bad idea that I couldn't believe I was actually okay with it. Come to think of it, I didn't verbally agree. I just sat in silence in our dark bedroom as Janine told me what she wanted to do.

It was so awful that I couldn't answer. So she took my silence as consent. I was too ashamed and too much of a wimp to stand up to my own wife.

Wimp.

You are a wimp. I remember hearing those words when I was growing up. The bigger boy next door bullied me for years. Finally, I went crying to my father. I told him what was going on. He told me to punch the bully in the mouth.

I told him I couldn't do that.

"You're a pussy," my father said to me. Of all the things he said to me over the years, it's the one I remember the most.

I stopped walking when I heard a group of voices outside. I stepped behind the couch and peeked out the window through the blinds. Just like I did when I was a kid, looking out for the thug next door.

Janine walked up the stairs to the townhouse, trailed by a pack of huge guys in hoodies and broad shoulders. Their voices were deep and guttural. Even without actually seeing them, I knew they were black. And since there were very few black students at our expensive private university, I knew they were members of the school football team.

She stopped on the top step and turned back to the gang. Even as she stood on the top step, she was not as tall as they were. She smiled, flirted, petted, whipped her hair out of her face and stroked it behind her ear.

All the things she always did when she saw me.

Janine tried to silence them all before inviting them in. The men's voices were loud and playful. And horny. The impetuosity of a group of students who were about to get laid.

For a second, I wondered how she had approached them about this opportunity. "Hey, guys! You guys want to come back to my house after practice and bang me? My professor husband doesn't mind at all!"

I wanted to hide when the front door opened, but I was too scared to move. So I ended up just standing behind the curtain as my wife led a group of huge football players up the stairs to our bedroom.

As the players walked by, I recognized some of their faces. Fortunately, I never had any of them in my classes. That would have been too much of a good thing. I made a mental note to make sure none of these guys attended any of my classes in the future. There was just no way I could sit through a lecture while looking out and knowing that one of the students had been with my wife. I saw her naked. They were touching her body. Her breasts and ass and pussy. Put his massive black cock deeper inside her than I ever could.

Anger rose in me even as I thought about it.

But there was something else. Pain. Excruciating pain as my rock hard cock tightened in my pants.

Visions of my wife being fucked by another man, a big black man, a group of big black men, turned me on like nothing else. What a pathetic embarrassment I was. I was not a man. I was a pussy. Just like father said.

When the last of the crew disappeared upstairs, I crept up behind them. I didn't want to miss a thing.

In our large master bedroom, Janine took off her shirt, unclasped her bra, slipped out of her pants and took off her socks. Her body was amazing. She was the center of attention. The pack of men, sweaty and swarming, circled around her.

I realized something I should have realized years ago. My wife loved being the center of attention. That's why she loved being an athlete. That's why she loved going to the games. She was an attention junkie.

It must have killed her to be with a boring old guy like me. The final straw must have been when I couldn't even get it up after she sucked my cock.

I could already tell that none of the guys watching her now had that problem.

Some of them were already naked. I couldn't help but marvel at their huge dangling hard and semi-hard cocks. Even semi-hard, they were at least twice the size of mine when I was fully erect. My God, one looked almost as big as Janine's forearm.

Others were still undressing, taking off their workout uniforms and sweatpants. They were straight from the gym, from working out. Their arms and legs were probably tired from shooting and running behind the ball.

Balls. These young black studs not only had the stereotypical huge black tails, but also balls that hung down like bulls at the fair.

And each of these lucky bastards was going to get a shot at my wife.

One of them opened our bathroom door and started to take a shower. He was already naked, and he stepped into the shower, but he was so big that he couldn't even fit under the shower head.

When he was done, he got out and wiped himself with a towel. But he left the water running and another climbed in. With the steam and the naked black men running around, they turned my suite into a locker room.

I thought about them using our shower. It was the shower where I watched the cascades of water pouring over Janine's firm butt. We lathered each other's hair, and she ran her fingers along my chest, and I squeezed her perky round tits, sucking and licking her hard pink nipples.

The first guy sauntered out of the bathroom with his chest shimmering and a towel wrapped around his waist. He had a chiseled, tattooed chest and arms. He looked so confident as he strode through my bedroom to my nearly naked wife. Like he owned the place instead of me!

He stood in front of Janine and dropped the towel to his feet. The massive table leg of a cock bounced around between his powerful thighs. He certainly wasn't shy about standing naked in front of all of us. Nor did he need to be.

Janine's eyes widened and she gasped when she saw the enormity of him. Janine had been with a few guys before we started dating, but I doubt any of the ones I knew looked like this guy. Or any of his teammates.

He grinned like that was exactly the reaction he expected from my pretty little white wife. With a quick sweep of his hands, he knocked Janine's unhooked bra off of her. The straps and cups spiraled around and slid to a point at my feet.

I picked it up and looked up just in time to see several hands reaching for Janine, grabbing her, clutching her, and finally throwing her onto our double bed. They tossed her onto the satin sheets where we fucked, writhed and exchanged breathless morning kisses. Before I took my beautiful Janine for granted.

I watched as big black hands descended on my wife's fair skin. Janine looked up at them. Her big eyes gave her an innocent look that I loved. She bit her lower lip again as different guys cupped her bare breasts. They fondled and squeezed them as if she were a piece of meat.

Then Janine's eyes darted to mine. She smiled and nodded at me.

My eyes locked on hers, and I caught myself nodding back. It was as if she had hypnotized me. I didn't want that to happen. I didn't want all these big black athletes gang banging my beautiful young wife. And yet, I stood there and gave my wife the okay. Go ahead, let the whole soccer team fuck you senseless on our bed.

But just then I slid into the big comfy chair in the corner. The chair I sat in and read while Janine fell asleep every night. Only this time my belt was unbuckled, and my pants and boxers were pulled down to my knees. And my shamefully small but stiff cock was in my hand.

On the bright side, I found a cure for my impotence, or ED, erectile dysfunction.... All I need to get a boner is a team of elite athletes screwing my wife. Maybe I could get my doctor to write a prescription for a soccer team.

It was around our first anniversary that Janine and I accidentally stumbled into this sexual discovery while watching porn together on my iPad one night. That night we watched a video of a cheerleader fucking five basketball players in a locker room. We've joked about it ever since. But I should have realized that there was a grain of truth behind the joke. For Janine, of course, but if I'm honest, it turned me on too. I just never imagined it was a fantasy we would experience firsthand.

At least until that fateful night when I couldn't get it up.

I tried to push the negative thoughts out of my head, at least for the moment. Whether I liked it or not, Janine was going to fuck these guys, so I might as well sit back and watch it happen.

The last member of the team came out of the steam-filled bathroom. Like the others, he was tall and slender, and his dark skin glistened with moisture.

As he stepped out of the bathroom, he looked over at me and sneered. He was the first to recognize my presence in the room.

I must have seemed pathetic to him, huddled in the corner of my own bedroom with my pants around my ankles. The nerdy white professor played with his tiny cock while he watched five big black studs fuck his pretty little wife in the ass.

Suddenly he yanked the towel off his hips. His long semi-hard cock dangled between his muscular thighs. My eyes were drawn to it. I couldn't help myself. I wasn't gay, but I was morbidly curious. I had to see what was deep inside my wife's cunt.

Just as I noticed his cock was darker than the rest of his skin, he must have caught me staring.

He turned around and hit me directly with the wet towel. It caught me right in the face. For a brief but brutal moment, I inhaled his musky, sweaty soccer player scent, only slightly masked by my Irish Spring soap.

Disgusted, I pulled the towel away from my face and noticed something in my mouth. I knew what it was as soon as I felt it. I stuck out my tongue and pulled a long, coarse, curly pubic hair away from my lips.

The basketball player laughed at me, and I was humiliated again.

I dropped back into my chair and turned my attention back to Janine on the bed. They had already begun to use her body for their own pleasure. My beautiful wife.

Monstrously large black hands were everywhere, grasping and clawing at her exposed flesh. There was so much going on that it took me a few seconds to realize that she was already on top of one of them.

Janine was basically sitting backwards on the man's lap. His foot-long cock was upright between her thighs. It was angled back against her, the shaft resting against her glistening, wet pussy. His huge hands clutched her lush breasts from behind.

A sickening feeling rose up inside me. The bile of hatred and jealousy swelled through my chest. Who were these guys to just come into my house and have their way with my wife? It wasn't fair. They could have any other woman, so why should they take mine.

But I was also rock hard, and one look at Janine's face told me she was in heaven. This was her greatest taboo fantasy come true. She had a big smile on her face. At least until the first massive ebony cock broke through her eager pink lips. Her face filled as her cheek expanded with the swollen head.

I averted my eyes, but they just darted between her legs. Janine's hand looked dainty and delicate as she stroked the long monster cock against her dripping pussy lips.

Then a massive hand covered hers, and together they guided the huge mushroom head into her tiny opening. I watched in horror as the monster pumped into her.

Janine spit out the other cock and cried out in pain. A trail of her saliva crossed her cheek and followed the other cock. She turned her head away, only to have another cock right in her face.

And so it began. The gangbang of my wife's school football team. Maybe they would make it an annual event.

So there was a long muscular black body under her, two behind her, and two in front of her. There were long dicks of varying girths and angles and shapes. Each of them was stiff and thrusting greedily at her, demanding her attention. After a few minutes they were all wet from her juices and saliva. Pure pure pure pure with wet sucking noises. Sucks and thrusts and smacks and more thrusts.

They took turns in her mouth and again in her cunt. It was like a team exercise at practice, and I wondered how many other pretty white coeds had been ravaged by this group before.

Janine had a mouthful of cock again. But this time two black hands held her head still as the huge soccer player poked her in the face. His cock was so big that Janine gagged as he fucked her flushed face.

Janine's fingers clawed into a thick brown bicep. The hands let go of her hair. Then another hand jerked her head back and she screamed.

I wanted to intervene and stop it. I was her husband, and I couldn't take it anymore. But I couldn't stand it. I couldn't stand it. Fear and shame overwhelmed me. I was not man enough to intervene. All I could do was watch them use my wife as a fuck doll.

Then I realized that Janine wasn't going to stop anything. Somehow she was lying on her back with her legs spread. Another guy was plowing into her with everything he had. Her thighs wobbled, and her body shook with each powerful thrust.

The image was so vivid in my mind. Every time he pounded into her, his big black balls bounced against her puckered asshole. But the other end worried me more. With his cock, he buried his balls deep inside my wife and kissed her hard on the lips. To my jealous eye, it looked like a really passionate kiss and not just a throwaway kiss.

Janine ground her hips into him. As she gyrated back and forth, her breath was ragged. She clutched him tightly as her orgasm overtook her. She cried out and bucked her hips as he continued to fuck her hard.

Her climax seemed to excite the entire team.

As I watched, all the dark-skinned guys blurred together. They were one sweaty, gushing black mass - a hard, wet, glistening black mass. Every now and then, Janine's pale skin would flash.

And that was when the first guy came inside her. He kept penetrating her wildly, filling her deeply with his seed.

He pulled out of her and was replaced by another pulsating cock.

Janine was spread wide on the bed as the second guy fucked her fiercely. Janine's naked breasts bounced in crazy circles as he pounded her again and again. Then he too exploded deep inside her.

Another guy sat on Janine's head and lowered his ball sack onto my wife's face. He pulled his ball sack over her nose until she sucked a ball between her lips. He pulled her hand to his cock, and he helped her stroke it.

Just as he was about to cum, he pulled back and shot his load into Janine's face. The thick whitish liquid splashed onto her cheek and over her nose. At first Janine's lips were cleaned, but he reached down and opened her mouth just in time to shoot another squirt onto her tongue. She swallowed involuntarily and giggled.

Several players changed positions around Janine. A hand tugged at her hair. Her neck jerked back. She bit her lower lip, staring with wide open eyes and dilated pupils. And another massive cock filled her. Big muscular athletic legs and thighs thrust and thrust.

"Ahhhhhhh." I wasn't even sure who was making the sound. The pounding of their bodies echoed through the room. The wild force startled me a little. How could he not hurt her?

But her hands didn't push him away. They clutched his skinny ass and begged him for more.

The pumping and thrusting gradually slowed. One man gave his last dying gasps. He grunted, closed his eyes and contorted his face. His body jerked, then he fell on top of them. A hand tapped him on the shoulder. Someone else was trying to get in.

"My turn, man."

No sooner had one pulled back than another took his place.

Two more guys finished the Janine missionary style that was always Janine's favorite. I was pretty sure one or both of them was screwing her for the second time, but I had lost track. They both came deep in Janine's gaping cunt.

All the while I was stroking my own pathetic little cock in the corner as I watched them use my wife for their pleasure. Big spent black bodies spread all over our bedroom. And my panting, naked Janine was right in the center of the action.

What were we doing? How did we get here?

But I couldn't be wrong. I knew exactly how we got there.

It's what we both wanted for so long. It's exactly what we had dreamed of. When we watched porn together, it was always the same. Every time. A cuckold video. With the same characters every time. A group of big, black bulls raping a sexy, slutty, cock-hungry white woman.

We were fascinated by the contrasts in skin color. We were seduced by the taboo, the forbidden, the undeniable sense of transgression that these scenes exuded.

And I longed to watch the submissive white husband take in the whole sordid spectacle, wide-eyed and hard cock in hand. Ashamed and humiliated as his wife was taken right in front of him. I took a perverse pleasure in my own sense of superiority over this pathetic husband in every video. How could he let them do that to his wife?

But my favorite part was always the clean up at the end. The husband was summoned to eat all the black semen from his wife's dripping pussy. The ultimate humiliation. They made the mess inside his wife; then they make him clean it up. They force him to taste every one of them, mixed with the aroused juices of the woman he loved.

Suddenly I was snapped out of my daze.

One of the big black bulls in my own bed beckoned me to join him.

I looked around as if I wasn't sure who he was waving at. " Me?"

"Yeah, man," he chuckled. "Come over here and get some."

I swallowed hard and stepped forward hesitantly.

"Check it out, man," he said to me. "Why would you ever share that?"

I looked at Janine as I thought of an answer. I wouldn't share it, I thought. But I wasn't the one making the decision. Janine did whatever she wanted, whether I liked it or not.

Janine wiped beads of sweat from her forehead and cheeks. Her skin had a damp sheen. The sweaty hair was matted down to her face. She smoothed it behind one ear. " Hold on tight," she said. She looked at me, then to the circle of boys. She pointed at me. "I want him to lick it out," she said.

" Damn. That bitch is whack," one of them said. They all laughed at the top of their lungs. All except Janine and me.

"Gross."

It was gross, but I still couldn't wait to get in there. Part of me was so ashamed of everything that was happening, but I was even more ashamed of this. This disgusting act I was about to do was turning me on more than anything. My cock felt like it was going to explode. I couldn't hold back much longer. It was so damn sensitive and hard it hurt.

They all backed away, clearing the way for me. It was such a strange moment, standing naked in the middle while Janine waved at me. As I approached Janine, I realized they were all hard and getting harder.

Janine smiled at me in that special way. That smile told me everything I needed to know. No matter how many big black bulls rammed their cocks into her, she still loved me.

She looked like a mess, a hot mess, lying on her back. She wiped the cum off her chest, off her lips and cheeks. She rubbed it into the sheets. She pulled a pillow under her head, spread her legs for me, and closed her eyes. Then she slid her hand down her chest and between her thighs and began rubbing her clit.

"Come on, man. Get in there."

"Yes, man. Eat that shit."

She opened her eyes and grinned at me. A final nod told me that was what she wanted. I climbed onto the bed between her legs. As I got closer, I saw a river of cum oozing from her stretched cunt. And I pinched.

I grabbed my cock and started fishing it into her.

"No," she said. Her tone was demanding and angry. She pushed my cock away with her hand. She kicked her heel into my thigh. "You know what to do," she said.

I felt weak, but I nodded.

"Eat me," she said, "I want you to lick me clean."

I felt a surge of new energy through my cock as it grew even harder. I leaned my face against her dripping pussy.

She reached out and put her hand on my head. She pressed my face into her gaping, dripping cunt. The warm liquid pressed against my chin and pursed my lips.

"Damn."

"Keep licking that shit!"

"This guy is disgusting."

Janine kept the pressure on my head, but she also raised her pelvis to my face.

"Stick out your tongue," she demanded, "lick it."

I did as I was told. I tasted the sticky warmth on my tongue. I choked. Once, and then a second time.

"Lick it up," she told me. "And swallow it."

I tried not to think about it, but I did as she said. I forced my tongue to suck her folds and even up to her cum splattered asshole. And finally I managed to swallow.

"Eat that shit, man. Eat the pussy." The soccer team laughed and roared, but I didn't care.

As I slurped between my thighs, I reached under myself and stroked my cock. I did the same. It was just too painful to ignore.

As my head bobbed between her thighs, I caught a glimpse of the circle around me. I couldn't believe my eyes. The naked, sweaty athletic bodies surrounded us. But the laughter and chatter died away. They stared at us and fondled each other. They jerked each other off.

For some reason, I took some satisfaction from the fact that they were jerking off. But there was no way I was going to be on the receiving end of their cumshots.

It was time, I decided. I pulled away from my wife, and she looked at me in surprise. She may have been about to have her own orgasm and didn't want to be interrupted. But I couldn't wait any longer.

I guided my small but stiff cock into her trembling cunt. I leaned into her and pushed as deep into her as I could. She felt much looser than usual, and I hoped it wasn't permanent.

Anyway, I grabbed her hand and pulled it to her clit. She was able to play with herself while I fucked her. As I thrust in and out, one of the players lurched to Janine's side. He stroked fast and furious, and his load exploded all over Janine's bouncing tits.

She smiled and spread the drops of cum over her skin with her free hand.

Another player joined in as the first finished, and he shot his load up under Janine's chin, and it pooled in the hollow just above her collarbone.

It was so exciting to watch each player squirt on my wife. I quickly reached my own climax as Janine began to tremble beneath me. Her cunt squeezed around my cock and her back arched. Her mouth opened as she moaned.

Suddenly, a huge black cock appeared at her lips. A bunch of hot sperm shot out of the mushroom head and disappeared into Janine's mouth. She closed her mouth and swallowed as another spurt splashed across her parted lips and cheek.

That was all I could take. My whole body spasmed as I came deep inside Janine. My release was such a relief as all my pent up tension just left my body. I was sure I had never felt so good before.

I pumped everything I had into my wife, and immediately after, I felt dizzy and collapsed on the Janine. The last thing I remembered was her arms around me. A gentle hand ran through my hair. I was so relaxed that I just let myself go.

It was still dark when I woke up. I was alone in the soaked bed, and my whole body was sore. I heard the shower running, so I got up and went to the bathroom.

The memory of what had happened that night rushed back into my mind. A whole new feeling of humiliation came over me. If word got out, my life would be ruined. I would be fired, and we would be run out of town.

But I tried to calm myself, knowing that Janine loved me no matter what. I took a deep breath before opening the bathroom door. I was about to jump in the shower with her, and we would clean our bodies together.

With a grin on my face, I opened the bathroom door and was met by a thick wall of steam. I walked toward the shower and pulled back the curtains.

Janine was in there, just as I expected.

What I hadn't expected were the two naked, tall, black soccer players who were in there with her. Janine was bent over between them, and the spray of hot water danced on her back. She was sucking the cock of the guy in front of her. The other guy behind her had his huge hands on her ass, spreading her cheeks apart. His thumb was ankle deep in her virgin asshole. His foot-long cock was buried in her cunt.

Immediately, I became hard again.

They pushed and pulled it back and forth. When the players saw me, they just grinned wide toothy grins. And continued to enjoy my wife.

In that humiliating moment, I realized something. I loved my wife, and I wanted her to be happy. If making Janine happy meant watching groups of big black men fuck her silly, then I had to do it.

Even though I was in my own house, in my own bedroom, I tiptoed away. Finally, I made my way to the guest bedroom. I climbed into bed and stared at the ceiling, listening for Janine.

After about an hour, the bedroom door opened easily. I saw the silhouette of my beautiful wife in the doorway. She was naked. My hard-on returned immediately. A good sign.

I pretended to be asleep. Only because I wasn't ready to talk about what had happened. When she lay down on the bed, I stayed still.

She climbed under the covers next to me. She whispered to me, "I love you, Frank."

I didn't answer, but I was still relieved to hear her say it.

Her hand slid to my side of the bed and didn't stop when it reached me. She found my hard cock and pushed back the covers.

My heart began to pound in my chest.

She pulled down my pajama bottoms and slid halfway down the bed. Her hand wrapped around my stiff little cock and stroked it gently.

Then my shaft was engulfed in a warm wetness that could only be her mouth. I closed my eyes in the darkness. All I could picture was all those big black cocks inside her.

I came in seconds and Janine swallowed every drop.

Despite my humiliation, I was happy as I fell asleep with my pretty wife in my arms. I knew I would be sharing my wife with big black men for a long time. And there was nothing I could do to stop that, even if I wanted to. I wasn't sure I wanted it. It made her happy, and it just turned me on too much. It was crazy.

And the craziness had just begun.

ANGELINA MOORE

WITH THE DELIVERY MEN

I look at the clock for the 4th time in as many minutes; it's almost time. My heart feels leaden in my chest; this is really going to happen soon.

She just got out of the shower and she looks damn good; the same sexy and sultry woman I married almost ten years ago. Her skin is glowing from the heat of the water as she enters our bedroom and wraps the terrycloth robe around her perfect, flawless body. Her breasts are just as high and full as the day I met her more than ten years ago. Her curves are more pronounced, fuller, and yet that makes her even more sensual.

Part of me goes numb, knowing that the reason we're here tonight is because this is a woman I clearly can't satisfy.

I try to hide a hint of skin as she closes the lush fabric around her, but she quickly closes it, rolls her eyes, and casts a disgusted glance in my direction where I sit gently on the edge of the bed.

"I thought we were past that, honey." She looks me square in the face with a cutting look I can't place; my eyes drop to the floor. This powerful, sexy woman stands before me, a pathetic excuse of a man, and strokes her lips with her tongue as she shakes her head in passive annoyance at me. Since when did she become like this? Since when did our social roles as dominant man and submissive woman change so much?

Probably when I admitted to both of us that I could not satisfy her, sexually, and that the solution was to allow her to seek that satisfaction elsewhere.

That brings us back to the present.

" Don't look until later, you know that."

I nod, already feeling chastised and submissive. Tonight is her night; tonight is for her pleasure.

She looks at her phone, an excited grin on her face. A knot of fear burns in the pit of my stomach; it's almost time.

I notice she's put on makeup in the bathroom, and her long red hair, though still damp, is pulled back in a sexy ponytail. I just love it like that, but tonight it's not for me.

No, tonight it's for him. Him, the man who will give my beautiful wife what she really needs that I can't give her: a big, strong cock.

He's been to the house before, twice actually, while delivering various packages. So we learned that our house was part of his normal route; that all the packages we ordered would be brought by him.

Much like tonight.

I had seen the way she looked at him, almost hiding it the first time, as she glanced down his crisp brown uniform over his thick arms and chest, tight and tight. Further down, the fabric seemed to hug what was clearly a sizable package between his legs. Even clothed, just looking at the pronounced bulge and the way he walked, you knew the man was really well endowed. I knew that night, one of my last attempts to please her in our bed,

that she was thinking about the fat package as I gently
fucked her.

The second time he came over, she stared at it
shamelessly, not caring if he or I noticed; we both did.

He is as arrogant as he is handsome. I can vividly
remember him smiling at me in my work clothes, shirt
and tie, as I made a futile attempt to bring in the last
large package she had ordered when it was delivered.
"Why don't you leave that to me, little guy," he had said
to me before simply hoisting the large box through our
front door. As he did so, he had also winked at her,
letting her - and me - know who the alpha male was.

She checks her phone again and I glance at the clock on
the nightstand; soon it will be time.

"Are you ready, honey?" She looks at me grimly, with
something hungry in her eyes, and I know she's thinking
about what's to come.

I just nod in affirmation and feel the cold fear, mixed
with the charging jolt of excitement, begin to build and

grow in my belly. She bites her lip and leaves the room, and I follow.

She wants me to watch from the den as she peers into the living room through a cracked door. There she will fuck him and from there I will watch as this cocky stud of a man takes my wife as she deserves. I will hide in the shadows like the morbid, chubby little slut that I am while she is treated like the goddess that she is.

As she leads me into the room, the telltale beep of a large truck backing up in the driveway sounds. Her eyes shoot open and she gasps for air; barely contained excitement is written all over her face as she hugs her robe tightly around her body.

"It's time." She bites her lip devilishly as she looks at me in the half-light of the cave.

Fear, shame, doubt flood my mind, but it's far too late for that. And then she kisses me quickly, chastely on the cheek, before pushing me into the room and closing the door almost all the way. As she leaves the room, I realize I've been holding my breath, and I let it out, shivering in the darkness of my vantage point.

Why am I here? Aside from the obvious - that I can't satisfy my wife with my out-of-shape body and pathetically average cock - why am I here? Why don't I allow her her dalliance and go out for the night? Drown my sorrows in a bar, drive around, think about something other than the love of my life being fucked and fucked by another man.

But I know; I'm here to watch this because I deserve it. It's not enough that she gets to be fucked by another man; I've denied her pleasure for ten years, and so I have to watch.

I hear the doorbell ring again, and then the front door opens. I can't make out any words, but I can hear her lilting laugh and his much deeper, gruff baritone. My tongue feels thick in my mouth as I strain, trying to hear a word. They speak for a minute; two. From where I stand there are no words, fearfully excited and disturbingly agitated, just muffled sounds and their laughter again.

Then they come closer, and I hear her just out of my sight, in the doorway to the living room. She takes a step back and barely enters my field of vision.

" So, do you think it will fit?" She hugs the robe close to her body, her completely naked body.

He chuckles deeply, "Oh, it will fit." And then deeper, "I'll make sure it fits perfectly, Stephanie."

How the hell does he know her name? I realize they're already closer than I even knew; this is the banter of two people who talked more than the two brief times he delivered packages. No, they talked more than that, which damn sure means he knew damn well what to expect here tonight.

And then she gasps dramatically and giggles. The son of a bitch knows she's married, he hit me, for Christ's sake.

And then come the words that make my blood run cold; the words that make my heart and gut drop through the floor.

"Sit tight Steph, we'll bring it right in."

We?!

As if I hear the voice screaming in my head, she turns to my hiding place behind the door, her eyes boring right into mine, even though I'm sure I'm hidden. And her eyes say it all: don't say a damn thing.

I feel a cold, creeping chill holding me in place. Us? As in, more than just him? She's not still going to go through with this, is she? What are they going to do, make the other guy wait in the truck?

And just like that, it hits me like a cold, sinking bag of rocks to the gut: she's going to have them both!

I feel the awful yet electrifying panic and excitement racing through my veins and a shiver runs down my spine. Did she plan this? Did she know there would be two of them? We had talked about the one; two is.... well, two is almost more than I can handle right now! I start pushing on the door.

But suddenly she's there, holding it, stopping me.

"No, no, honey." She whispers at me through the crack, her voice low and dripping with lust.

"You just stay there, okay?"

I start to panic again. "But... But..."

"Shhhh... there you go, baby. Just stay in your hiding place and watch. Ok?" She blows me a kiss, and then muffled voices come in from the hallway, and she pulls away from me.

She knew all along. The thought stuns me, and yet my cock is almost painfully hard in my pants. Then my hand drops to the doorknob, and I feel my breath come quickly as I approach the crack in the door and peer through it.

They fidget and grunt as they maneuver the new couch into the room. A damn couch, how could I have assumed only one guy would deliver it? Of course, there are two men.

And as I size them up, I feel a flash of something - jealousy, perhaps? Excitement? - It rushes through me.The two big delivery guys are built like bodybuilders; tan uniforms stretched tight across thick, powerful chests and shoulders and around bulging biceps as they maneuver the couch into the living room. My stomach sinks as I imagine what else they'll be handling before my eyes.

There's the one we know, the one who made me feel like a wimp during the last delivery. He's blond, handsome in the university-student way I've never felt. A chiseled, strong jaw, a white smile, and a dark look in his eyes. I grit my teeth and think about the last time he was here; the way he stood his ground with me, the way he openly judged my wife right in front of me.

The other man is older, though he's built the same way and looks good outdoors in that way. A thick black beard covers his chin, matching his hair, and I notice the sleeve of tattoos running down one of his arms under his short-sleeved uniform. I know, just by knowing her as long as I have, that deep down it's men like this who are just her type. I look at her, my wife, standing there in just her bathrobe, and I can almost see her shaking with excitement. Seeing her like this excites me, and I can feel my cock aching in my pants.

"You can just put it there, men."

They set the new couch down; it's directly across from the study door, facing me. As they pulled back from the couch, the dark-haired man reached his arm back and knocked the collection of things onto a shelf next to the fireplace. With a thud, my bowling trophy crashed to the floor.

Yes, I have a fucking bowling trophy; it's even fucking displayed like it's a thing that needs to be shown off. Jesus, no wonder we're in this scenario where I'm hiding in the dark like a pussy, watching two real men give my wife the fuck she needs.

The man starts to apologize before she stops him.

"Oh, please, don't worry about it. It's just my husband, and for heaven's sake, it's a bowling trophy."

The two men snicker as she taunts me, and the older one responsible for the smashed trophy kicks her contemptuously with his boot as they laugh at my expense.

The dark-haired man, still chuckling, says something about "papers" that I don't quite understand, and leaves the room, presumably for the van. The younger blond guy stays, and then it's just the two of them.

For a moment, my fear subsides; maybe she has just the one after all! Maybe a furtive look was exchanged between the two men that I missed, where the older one got the hint to run off and let his friend fuck the housewife. Shakily, I take a breath; it's the only one, and the one I think I might be able to handle at the moment.

And then, as he turns to straighten a side table he bumped into on the way in, without any preamble, without having spoken a word, she unties the knot at the front of her robe. It falls open in the middle, revealing a full breast and her perfectly waxed, flushed pink pussy. Jealousy floods me hotly; she never fully exposed herself, even when I asked her to! And yet she has prepared her pussy perfectly for this stud!

The younger man turns back to her, and then he freezes. His eyes suck into my wife's exposed body, and I see a dark hunger flash across his face.

My first instinct is to be angry or offended at his lustful looks, at the way his eyes stare at my wife. But her face is flushed pink, her breasts rising and falling with each breath, and I know she's probably dripping wet by now as she does this. I have to remind myself that we are here, right here, because of my shortcomings as a husband and as a man.

I look back at the younger stud's face and see the raw desire there, and my jealousy and crushing fear are temporarily replaced by something else; is it pride?

"Do you like what you see?" She smiles at him.

I feel a rush; she's never been so sexually open, so slutty with me. I also notice that her whole tone is different. With me, she's always so sharp, so biting and dominant. And yet, here, with this hot young guy sizing her up with his eyes and chiseled good looks, she sounds almost submissive; like she's shyly seeking his approval.

He grins at her, almost as if sizing up whether or not she's going to mess with him. But now I know, now I'm sure he knew what he was getting when he came to her. He doesn't try to figure out her motives, he just gets drunk on her perfect body. His eyes are glued to her exposed cunt, neatly waxed and on display for him.

"I think I see a lot I like." His eyes flash; he stares at her pussy as he talks to her.

"I thought you had a husband."

"Does it matter?"

I wince and moan; God, she's acting like a whore!

"Not to me." He moves toward her now, grinning that cocky grin, and she opens her robe wider, exposing herself completely to this other man.

"Looks like I'm missing out on the fun."

My stomach drops through the floor again. The same cold dread from earlier grips me; the other man is back.

My eyes dart to the living room door and see him standing there, a scowl on his face. He chuckles as he enters, his eyes fixed on my wife's perfect tits, her body naked and exposed. I can almost feel the heat and tension in the room rising, in unison with the pounding pulse in my ears.

This is really happening; My wife for almost a decade is really about to fuck them both, right before my eyes!

My heart is racing now as the eyes of the two men roam over my wife's body. Part of me is screaming inside, screaming how crazy this is and how far beyond what we have talked about, even now! And yet, as I look at her and see the raw lust and desire flashing through her face, I see looks I haven't seen in a long, long time. I know that all of this is because of me.

I look at the two big studs judging her in size, her eyes fixed on my wife....

...And we are here because of me.

"I was just asking your friend here if he liked what he saw." She arches her chest outward, her perfect pink nipples stretching proud and erect from her tits. Then she shakes the robe off her shoulders, and she stands before the messengers completely naked.

I have blood plugs in my ears and my pulse is racing. The men nod and giggle; their eyes roam freely up and down her body, from the nipples high on her full breasts to the wetness now obviously glistening between her legs in the light of the room.

"Well, I definitely like what I see." The older man nods and grins as he moves toward her. I feel my breath catch, knowing I'm about to watch another man lay his hands on my wife.

"Maybe you need a closer look?" She smiles at the man moving across the room toward her, her hips cocked in a sinfully slutty way as she moves her legs apart and exposes herself to them. Her arms are crossed behind her back, making her look so submissive, so eager to please them.

They both move toward her, both much larger than her smaller frame; they tower over her and are certainly bigger and stronger than me. They approach her, like two wild animals circling a prey, until they are right in front of her; so close that I know they can smell the shampoo in her hair, probably the arousal between her legs. Her face is flushed and looks wild as the two stallions approach her.

And then she grabs the cocky young guy by the collar of his shirt and presses her lips hotly to his mouth. Hungrily, he rubs himself tightly against her, his hand sliding over the soft, exposed skin of her belly. Behind her, the older man growls and moves toward her. He grinds close behind her, against her, biting her neck.

A burning, fiery sensation burns in my belly, threatening to tear me apart at any moment as I watch this. I tense and clench my hands at my side, barely breathing as I watch these two large men tear and devour my wife, running their hands over her naked body.

I should be angry; I know that. I should be banging on the door to physically tear them away from her and assert myself as a man and as a husband.

But that's not going to happen; I know that. She wants that; it's written boldly on her face, in an expression of raw ecstasy, and I'm not going to be the one to take it away.

As if I even could.

She moans loudly into the blond man's mouth as her hands slide over the thick bulge in his pants. She fumbles with his belt buckle and yanks at the zipper of his tight brown uniform. I hear her cooing and whimpering as her hands dip inside to his cock. Without another thought, my own hand drops to the front of my pants and I begin to stroke my throbbing erection through the fabric.

She frantically pulls down his pants, and I gasp as his cock pops out and presses against her thigh with a thick, audible slap. She takes a sharp breath as his throbbing erection hits her skin, bringing her hand to her mouth in shock.

I was right, this guy is fucking huge! To say he's bigger than me would be an understatement to say the least. He's easily twice my size in girth and length. Even the shape of his cock, the way it proudly curves into a round, jutting knob, dwarfs my own pointy dick. My erection almost sways in my pants at the sheer size of this hung stud, running his hands over my wife's tits as he presses his big cock against her skin.

Her hands tentatively reach down to him. Her fingers close over him, but don't quite reach around his girth, and my mouth goes dry. Slowly she strokes him against her thigh as she presses her lips back against his, caressing his big strong hands and pulling on her heavy breasts.

The man behind her has removed his belt and is also pulling down his uniform. With a sharp THWACK sound, his own throbbing cock pops out of his pants and slaps against the soft curve of my wife's ass. I groan and feel the blood rush through my veins; he's just as big as the first guy! I wonder briefly if a big cock is a prerequisite for getting a job at the delivery company.

She's moaning erotically now, those super sexy little squawking sounds I've never heard from her before. She reaches for the guy behind her, and then she's visibly shaking, eyes closed as she holds both of their cocks in little hands and strokes them back and forth against her skin.

I shamefully rub my own skinny erection through my
khakis,

They are now pushing her back and moving her towards
the couch they just brought into my house and bought
with my credit card. She is pushed into a sitting position
in front of them, her chest flushed and heaving, her legs
spread lewdly.

The two men take off the rest of their uniforms and,
from my hiding place, expose their bodies to me. Jesus,
they are fucking perfect specimens of anatomy;
muscular and lean, muscles defined across the chest and
shoulders in a way I never was, not even at my most
athletic in college when we met.

Looking at her, I realize how truly pathetic and shameful
it is that she has stayed with me as long as she has.
Taking in her body, her hard muscles, her huge cocks, I
begin to piece together the little hints, the comments
and suggestions I've gotten from her over the years.
Slowly, right there in the dark, the pieces come together
to show that these are the kind of men - real men - she
craves.

The man with the beard and his tattoos; I suddenly
think of all the times she's wanted to go to that
particularly hip bar downtown for a drink when we
decide to go out. That's the place where the guy with all
the tattoos on his arms and neck works on Fridays; the
one who always just charges us for my drinks.

I think of the guy who does our tree and hedge work,
with the big hairy beard and the cheeky smile. I used to
make fun of his grizzled lumberjack look, but now that I
think about it, I'm not sure she ever really laughed back.
It was always more of a conciliatory giggle to appease
me. The whole time she didn't think of him as
unattractive at all!

Every good looking guy on TV, in magazines, in real
life; every single guy that defines that "manly" look that
I never was, that she always said she didn't like.

I know now that all of that was a goddamn barbed lie; a
lie to make me feel better, sure, but a lie. That hurts.

Over by the couch, the men are naked now, stroking
their fat cocks as they go down on my wife. She rubs her
pussy like a slut, and as they approach her, she reaches

up and rubs her wet, sticky fingers over their pulsing lengths.

And just like that, she opens her mouth and wraps her lips around the younger blonde guy. Just like that, I watch as my wife opens her mouth and gives another man a blowjob.

And I've never been so aroused.

She moans ecstatically at the first contact of this new meat on her mouth, and she immediately gets off on it. She moans loudly and animalistically like a whore and starts pushing her mouth down his length as far as it will go. She gags around him, her lips spreading obscenely wide as she wildly fucks his cock with her mouth, an expression of pure lust on her face.

I can't even believe what I'm witnessing! I have always loved her blowjobs, - loved them - but they are always tender, loving. She's licked me and licked me, made me come naturally, but she's never done anything so....so primal and voracious as this! And I realize that because this is what she wants, to be used like a disposable slut by a strong alpha stud with a huge fucking cock.

The older man strokes himself as he presses the thick head of his cock against her cheek. Gasping, she pulls the blond off and spits obscenely from her lips onto his striking red cock before turning around and almost inhaling the other cock. She slurps on his cock, gargling with her own spit as she swallows it, barely getting halfway down his cock before she pulls off, gasping for air.

I frantically rip my pants open now and push them around my ankles like a naughty, spanish schoolboy as I reach for my puny but painfully hard cock. I let spit drip into my palm as I cover my 10cm cock with my fist and start stroking hard and fast, trying to imagine that it's me pushing my cock down her throat.

She's so fucking sexy; one hand is buried in her dripping wet pussy while the other is stroking a big cock while she sucks and gurgles on the other. From time to time she switches, each time drooling more spit and pre-cum from her slutty mouth onto her tits and down her thick shafts to the heavy balls below.

I'm stroking harder now, knowing I'm already close because I'm gasping and probably making too much noise, but I don't care because all I want at this moment is to come. I just want to cum and watch my wife be a total slut to these two men.

And then just like that, just as I'm getting ready to explode, I lose my footing. I take a quick step and try to regain my balance, but my pants and underwear are still knotted and twisted around my ankles. And then I lurch toward the door, and with no time to make a single sound except a high-pitched "whoop" like a little girl, I catapult myself through the door and crash into the living room.

Stephanie gasps heavily as she jerks her head back from the thick cock buried in her throat. The two suppliers turn sharply in the direction of the sound as I crash into the room, but they make no move to cover themselves or move away from my wife. My wife, with her hands around their dicks, and drool and pre-cum dripping in sticky strands onto both of their shafts.

The blond guy recognizes me immediately, of course, and he chuckles.

"Well... Shit, look who's been spying." The older guy looks at me funny, but when the blond guy elbows him, it's like he suddenly gets it.

"Is that the husband?" His voice is a much deeper baritone, raspy, and sounds totally masculine. I have full confidence in the world that any sound he made as he stumbled through a door, as if he would ever be in that position, would be absolutely nothing compared to the girlishly bitchy sound I made as I stumbled in.

Steph is snorting now, obviously pissed that I interrupted her. She sighs dramatically.

"Honey, I told you you could watch from the study!"

The men are laughing at me now as I carefully rise from the floor. My pants are still knotted and twisted at my feet, my doughy, cheesy body half on display and my semi-hard, pathetic excuse of a slightly dangling cock. Both men still have rock hard erections, and the blond guy even starts to slowly stroke his as he watches me stand up.

"So... that's why you need some real cocks, huh?" he looks down at Stephanie, who blushes furiously. In her silence, I realize that part of the whole thing with this, part of this whole appeal to her is that I'm just kind of there. It's like when I'm there, she suddenly has a lot less confidence in what she's doing. I'm the horrible reminder of what a bitch she is.

" The older man strokes his thick beard, his hairy, defined chest and tattooed arms ripple. " This little bitch is so bad you need two dicks to make it all better?"

"I... I..." She's blood red now, her confidence gone as she looks down at the floor.

"He asked you a question, bitch." The blonde man's sharp instruction brings her eyes up quickly, along with a gasp on her lips. Suddenly I see the fire from earlier flare up in her eyes, that untamed lustful desire.

"Yes... Yes."

"Yeah, what."

She swallows hard, her big eyes glowing in her lust, her chest heaving and her nipples pink and erect.

"Yes, I need two big cocks to satisfy me because my little groveling husband can't."

The breath goes out of my chest sharply at her words. We both knew that; hell, that's why we're here. But to hear it said like that; wow.

The two vendors grin at each other.

"Why don't you help us show your little man here how you need to be treated, honey?"

The older man presses his cockhead against her cheek as he strokes himself, arms tight and corded. She flinches for a second, but then her eyes meet mine. And then she instantly opens her mouth and sucks him in as her gaze bores into mine.

"There you go. Good girl." The blonde guy now turns back to her, stroking his cock and reaching down to fondle her tits. She moans deeply again, clearly reveling in being treated this way. Suddenly I realize that they are not paying any attention to me; it occurs to me that I should leave, or at least retire to the study where I am supposed to be.

I start shuffling awkwardly toward the door when the older man's voice stops me.

"You wait here and keep watch, bitch."

I freeze and slowly turn around. The big bearded guy stares at me with a sharp look and cuts me down. Immediately I feel like I've let him down, like I've let him down. The fact that my wife's mouth is wrapped around his cock makes this feeling interesting.

"You don't sit, you don't close your eyes, you just watch." He grins as Stephanie noisily pulls off his cock, choking and sputtering before turning to the blonde guy and sucking his balls into her mouth.

"I don't want you to look away for once, you understand? No matter what you see, no matter what we do to your little bitch of a wife, you don't fucking move, you understand me?" His face is rock hard, demanding my compliance; I nod.

Just as he's about to take my wife's body, he's taken the last meager shred of my dignity; I belong to him, too.

I stand like a fool a few feet away, my pants still ridiculously bunched around my ankles. I start to take off my shirt, thinking maybe I should be naked too, but when I see their hard, toned bodies, I suddenly become aware of myself, and I leave it on.

Instead, I just put my hand around my cock. The bearded man is watching me, and I look at him, almost asking for permission to stroke my pathetically inferior cock as he and his friend turn my wife into a cock-addicted slut. He just snorts and shrugs.

"Fine."

"Oh God, I need one of those in my pussy right now!" She moans and whimpers while fucking her mouth like a slut. As she says this, the dark haired man gets a hard look in his eyes. He reaches down and yanks on her ponytail, pulling her head back. She gasps at the roughness; the blond guy just grins.

"Listen, you cock-hungry little bitch," the bearded, tattooed guy growls at her. "We're here because you need those big, fat cocks because that little limp dick over there," he nods at me, my cock standing erect as he grabs my wife.

"That little limp dick over there can't take care of you." His hand grips his cock, and he smacks Stephanie across the lips with it, following it across her flushed and surprised face.

"But if you want this cock," he gives her another light slap on the cheek, this time with his heavy, meaty cock; "you listen to what we say and do exactly what we tell you. Is that clear?"

Stephanie nods up and down quickly. God, she looks so lustful, so desperate for these men. She doesn't even meet his eyes as he talks to her; instead, her gaze is glued to his swaying cock, with a hungry, lustful look in her eyes.

"Yes." She whimpers out.

"Yes, what?" He's still holding her ponytail. Slowly she looks up at him, her eyes glowing with lust.

"Yes, my lord."

And just like that, these men own my wife.

The bearded man smiles. "Good, now suck his cock, and I want to see you mean it, girl." He pushes her toward the cocky blond guy, who eagerly grabs her ponytail and guides his throbbing cock to her hungry open mouth. He moans as her lips close tightly around him, lapping at his crown before it slides wetly and noisily down his shaft.

I can't even help myself; without even thinking, I drop my hand to my lap and wrap a few fingers around my cock. The bearded guy sees me, though, and laughs darkly.

"Look at your man, bitch. Look at him over there jerking his little cock like he's watching porn or something." She mumbles around the blond's cock as the older man begins to pull her pelvis sideways, dragging her across the couch until she's draped over it. One leg is splayed off to one side, lewdly exposing her glistening pink cunt as she eagerly bobs her mouth up and down on the blond guy's cock.

"Is this the kind of man you want? The kind of man who jerks off when his own wife is being fucked by two other men?" The bearded guy snorts, and then he bends over and squats low between my wife's spread legs. He presses his huge cock against her pussy lips and lets it rest there. I can see her eyes roll back in her head as she trembles. She wants this.

"You watch yourself, little man, because I'm going to ruin your wife for you." He looks me full in the face without flinching, looking like some kind of conquering Viking with his smoky dark eyes and big beard; his huge muscular chest and arms. The thick club of a cock nestles right between my wife's pussy lips.

"If she wasn't happy with your cock before, she'll never want anything less than this," he taps his head against her clit, making her moan at the thick girth in her throat. "When we're done with her. Don't look away."

And then he pushes her in, his huge cockhead straddling her cunt, slowly spreading and stretching her wide as he presses her into the sticky, wet folds.

For a moment I can't believe he's actually going to penetrate her with that thing. It's just too big! But then, with an almost unearthly muffled cry of pleasure from my wife's lips, his head dips into her pussy and he starts sliding in.

He takes it slow but steady as he thrusts inch by inch, having put huge inches of his cock deep inside her. It's almost surreal to watch something so big slide into such a tight little hole; I couldn't look away if I tried! She's howling like a whore the whole time, one hand playing wildly with her clit while the other hand is wrapped around half the shaft in her mouth, unable to get past her lips.

And just like that my wife, my partner for more than a decade, is filled from both ends like a spit roasted slut. She is completely filled with two huge cocks, and neither of them is mine. I am horrified, ashamed, emasculated....

yet insanely aroused, all at once. I can think of nothing but the burning need to see them fuck her senseless. I want them to take things as far as they can, to use them in every way possible, to own them. I want to watch them fill her holes, cum in her, on her, and turn her into a cum eating slut, desperately addicted to big cocks.

I want all that, knowing I can't do it myself.

But I watch.

The bearded man buries his cock and balls deep inside my wife; fucking her and stretching her in ways I will never, ever be able to satisfy. From my vantage point, I can watch as he impales her fully. I can see the way her lips suck and grip his girth as he pushes his fat cock deep into her pussy.

Suddenly I realize he's not wearing a condom; he's inside my wife without a rubber! Suddenly I imagine him filling my wife's pussy with his cum; creaming her until this stud's thick jizz drips out of her. The thought drives me wild and I stand there fisting my cock all the harder.

The blond guy just giggles and watches me jerk off
pathetically while he literally fucks my wife's mouth. He
has both hands on her ponytail, gripping it like a handle
as he puts her mouth over and over on his cock like he's
fucking a pussy.

He pulls her off him, gasping and drooling, she spews
spit and precum, a look of absolute ecstasy, a look of
pure, unbridled lust across her face. I stare at this
woman I've known for a decade, spent a third of my life
with, and realize I barely know her; I've never seen this
look, not in 10 years.

"So, how do you like the big cock so far, honey?"

"I love it!" She gasps loudly, practically yelling the
words. Her face and chest are bright red and flushed,
and her eyes are rolling wildly in her head as the bearded
guy pounds her pussy.

"You what, slut?"

"I love him, sir!"

He's putting even more pressure on her now, knowing exactly what to say to make her squirm like this. How long has he known her now, 20 minutes? And he's already made her submissive, made her do his will, worship him and obey him. I'm her fucking husband, and she's never treated me like this, never spoken to me in this begging, sexually submissive way. The thought burns me, nags at me, but seeing her like this makes me gasp.

"What do you love?"

"I love big cocks!"

"And does your husband have what you need?"

" No, oh God, no," she moans orgasmically, and I watch her face tense as her own climax rips through her body as the huge cocks of the suppliers bounce in and out of her.

" Do you want those big cocks filling your holes while your husband watches?"

"Yes! Oh please! Please fuck me with your big - ugh! - HUGE cocks!"

I don't know this woman anymore! Not even an hour ago I lived in this house with my wife; but this moaning, squirming slut who comes like a whore while two big fat boners fill her pussy and mouth is someone brand new. This scares me and excites me like crazy.

The blonde guy has his cock back in her throat and fucks her mouth while she jerks his shaft. The bearded guy grunts and clings to her, his tight grip leaving bruises on her that I will see for days to come.

"I'm gonna cum, girl, and I'm not backing off." He turns and grins at me, "Did you hear that? I want you to watch closely, bitch. Watch me fuck your wife's tight little pussy with my big cock, and watch me fill it with my cum. If you ever get to fuck that pussy again, I want you to think about it; I want you to think about me filling her with my cum."

And then with a grunt, he buries his balls deep, all the way into my wife, without a condom. He screams, and suddenly she's writhing under him and I know he's coming. I know he's filling her, his huge balls emptying their mighty load into my wife, marking her as his own.

Right after that, the blond guy grunts and I hear Stephanie choke and suffocate. I see her eyes bulge in her head, her cheeks and throat pumping as she swallows his load. He jerks out, jerking his wet and throbbing shaft, pumping strand after strand of cum all over her upturned face. Her mouth is wide open, tongue thrust out, wagging furiously and desperately to taste his gift.

And just like that, watching two men cum all over and deep inside my wife, watching two OTHER MEN, two bigger, stronger, more dominant and better men fuck my wife, how she needs to be treated, how I can never treat her:

I cum.

It is pathetic and humiliating. Both men, along with my cum-soaked wife, watch me with awkward expressions on their faces as I grunt and angrily fist my cock while cum drips off the end and down my fingers and onto the pants clenched around my feet. I close my eyes and feel the shame wash over me and a drop splashes down my belly.

Then I hear them - all three of them - laughing. I open my eyes to see my wife sucking idly on the blond's cock tip as the older man slowly jerks his huge cock against her red and stretched looking cunt. White sperm drips out of her; another man's sperm - the sperm of two other men! - flows freely from my wife's pussy, out of her mouth and all over her face. And I'm standing in the middle of my own living room watching, with cum on my hand and on my pants.

"Okay, honey, I think you're done, okay?" She says it in such a belittling, scolding way. My cock is already wilting in my hand, and I enviously notice that the two delivery men are still rock hard.

They are not done with my wife yet.

While I stand there and my cock drips with sperm while limping, they are already standing and switching. The bearded older guy moves to her mouth while the cocky blond guy moves between her legs and strokes himself while looking at her dripping and sticky cunt.

"Why don't you go wait upstairs while we take care of her down here." The older man chuckles at me and slowly pumps his thick erection while my wife bends her head to press on his balls.

"Unless you want a taste too?"

I'm rooted to the spot, staring awkwardly at his cock. He's not serious, is he? Is that what he really wants? I'm stunned, petrified, and scared. Mostly, I start to realize that if he - the alpha - tells me to do it, I will.

Then they both laugh out loud at me. My wife rolls her eyes at me as if I've made a faux pas at a cocktail party. That frozen second is broken, my shame and humility ended. I turn and shuffle out of the room, red-faced, my pants still around my ankles.

Upstairs in our bed, I toss and turn, trying to sleep, but also hearing her orgasmic cries from below. It's late and I'm exhausted and drained, but I'm trying to get my dick hard again just so I can jerk off. And then, just when I think I might be able to get up again, if only to jerk off to the sound of my wife being fucked by two other men, the door to the bedroom opens.

For one, brief second, I think that maybe they're gone; that she's done and it's out of her system and she's come back to me.

No.

They enter, all three of them, and she actually bounces up and down on the blond man's thick tail as he carries her in. He throws her on the bed - our fucking marital bed! - right next to me and just keeps fucking her. She ignores me like she doesn't even know I'm there as her cacophony booms through the room.

"Fuck off, buddy."

The bearded guy nods for me to get out of bed as he begins to shuffle onto the bed, and I obey. I quickly scurry to the chair across from them.

There I spend the rest of the night; huddled in the chair, futilely stroking my semi-hard cock as they fuck and use my wife in every way possible.

Around dawn, I am awakened by Stephanie.

"Are you coming to bed?"

I rub my bleary eyes, light filters in through the
windows, and the men are gone. Stephanie is a mess, her
hair is a mess, her lipstick is smeared all over her lips.
She is naked, and she beckons me to the bed.

Eagerly, I jump behind her, life rushing into my sore
cock as I press against her.

"No... no, honey, I'm too sore. Not tonight."

Frustrated, I grit my teeth.

"Tomorrow?"

She sighs sleepily; "probably not."

"Well, when then?"

"Oh, I don't know, I'm tired." She closes her eyes and burrows into the pillows.

Oh fuck. I realize that my fears have been confirmed; that she is now completely addicted to big dicks. She'll never want mine again.

"Just hold me, ok?"

Good, at least that's what I'm still good for as a husband, I guess. I wrap my arms around my wife and pull her tightly against me. And then I freeze.

She's still completely covered in her cum; she hasn't even showered yet! It's sticky and wet all over her back as I press against her, and I feel it all over me, from my cock to my chest! Revulsion washes over me coldly, and I start to pull back.

She grips my arms tightly and holds me.

"No-no, cuckold." She grins wickedly with her eyes
closed and whispers it to me.

"That's what you're good for, so stay put."

And I do.

Because I know she's right.

ANGELINA MOORE

MY WIFE'S FIRST DATE

It was a Friday night, and the hotel restaurant was packed, and there was a buzz in the air. This was one of the few hip places downtown. Beautiful people from all over the world came here. So I didn't think anyone we knew would be there. It was a safe place for us to meet my wife's date.

Pop music and funky techno mashups blasted from the speakers. The heavy bass vibrated through my entire body, only adding to the tension that was already building inside me. And from the minute Jana and I entered the fancy place, I noticed an intense energy emanating from her. She was practically humming with excitement. It was a feeling I had never gotten from her before, and I knew she was hungry to see her big, black younger stud. We saw him sitting alone at the bar sipping a bottle of beer.

She had found him through an app or something. It didn't take long for her to find him. It had been barely a week since I had agreed to go along. It had occurred to me that she had been planning this meeting for longer than she had let on.

Not that it mattered, I guess. If that was what she needed to keep our marriage going, then that was what was going to happen. I loved her too much to let her go, and she usually made me feel the same way.

So that's how we got so far out of our comfort zone. Farther from mine than hers in the end, I guess.

Before she approached him, she took a deep breath. I had taught her that in my days as a speaker. As always, it seemed to work, and she calmed down. At least it seemed that way from the outside.

If she felt what I felt, then no amount of controlled breathing would make her completely calm down. Sex with a stranger has that effect on a person. As far as I knew.

Just when I thought she was getting close, she slipped into an alcove by the restrooms. In the shadows, she pulled her pocket mirror out of her purse, combed her long white-tipped fingernails through her long hair, and reapplied her slutty red lipstick. Finally, after her pit stop, she seemed ready to meet him. Ready for anything that might happen.

In a different setting, I might have whispered a few words of encouragement. But this was no ordinary meet and greet. More like meet and fuck. And I couldn't trust myself to say anything even close to the right thing. "Go get 'em!" or "You can do it!" or "I'm rooting for you!" didn't seem quite appropriate for a situation where I was delivering my wife into the arms of another man.

Not that she needed the encouragement. Despite her fears, she was looking forward to it like I'd never seen her look forward to it before.

Not even on our wedding day.

She barely noticed my presence as she nervously walked to the bar. I still wasn't quite sure what they had to say to each other. "Hello, I'm Jana, and this is Thomas, my wimpy husband who can't satisfy me, and that's why I crave your huge, black, anaconda-sized cock".

In the car on the way there, she was also worried about what people in the restaurant might think. That somehow everyone might notice that we were there for them to have sex with a stranger. That she might be mistaken for a prostitute or something. Who knows what she was thinking?

It annoyed me that she was more concerned about what random nobodies would think than she was about her husband of seven years.

Jana was a virgin when we met, and never really went through the meat market scene. So she had no experience approaching relative strangers in a bar. Thank goodness.

I was much more concerned about the racial aspects. I always thought I was open-minded to people of other races. But that was an abstract thing. It was a very different thing to allow a person of another race to fuck my wife.

Suddenly we were on the move. Or Jana was on the move. I just followed in her wake as she swayed through the crowd. Every guy she passed looked at her, some more openly than others. No one even looked at me.

It was actually amusing to see a guy's face light up for the half second he thought she was coming over to him. Only to see that same face go slack as hope faded into reality.

All too soon, we were at the bar. Her "date" was sitting with his back to us. I thought we were sneaking up on him when I realized he was watching us in the mirror behind the bar. He must have liked what he saw because of his sly grin.

He didn't let on that he knew we were there. Jana patted him on the shoulder. He turned around, all calm and confident. As if beautiful women were constantly coming up to him and begging him to take them to bed with him.

But as cool as he was, he couldn't help but smile at the sight of Jana. She was a feast for the eyes with her little black neckline revealing her dress. It still fit her all these years later, maybe a little tighter in the chest. She had replaced her doe-eyed innocence with the sexiness of a grown woman, and it was stunning.

He introduced himself as he got up from the bar stool. They embraced and she gave him a kiss on the cheek as he leaned down to her. His smile remained as he lowered his eyes and sneaked a peek at her chest.

Jana seemed to relax a little after they touched. Almost as if she had grounded herself and discharged the extra energy.

"David, this is my husband," Jana said, inflating her body to include me.

My hand was dwarfed in his and he almost pushed me to my knees with his iron grip. "You're a very lucky man," David said.

Not as lucky as he was.

They found a table while I tried to get the feeling back in my hand. It was a hand I expected to need later in the evening.

I sat quietly like a naughty child in the corner of the table while the adults talked. They ordered and started chatting.

"I was really glad you came tonight," David said. "You're definitely even more beautiful in person."

"You're cute," Jana replied, blushing.

"No, that's true. Most people look better in the app. But not you. It was really refreshing."

Jana stared at him and sipped her Sex On The Beach without replying. It was obvious she was enjoying the praise he heaped on her. Something to definitely do more of.

She continued to smile as if she was more than pleased with his appearance. I was, to a certain extent. He looked more like a professional athlete out on the town than the nasty gang member I was expecting.

At that moment Jana was shaking and smiling, no doubt thinking of all the things he would do to her body.

David stood up and took off his jacket. He draped it around my wife's shoulders. Like a true gentleman. While I sat there like a fool.

"Why are you smiling?" he asked as he sat back down. "You must think I'm old-fashioned, but a lady should be treated like a lady."

"No, why do you say that?" asked Jana, reaching across the table and placing her hand on his.

"I don't know, being so young and all. It's just the way I was raised, I guess."

He laid it on pretty thick. But Jana gobbled it up.

"I didn't think I was your type. You probably go for guys who are older and more sophisticated."

Jana shrugged and shook her head. "No, I only like guys who are nice and sweet and like to be with women."

"Well, I definitely like being with women," David said and they both laughed. This guy probably bangs more girls in one weekend than I've had in my entire life.

Jana lowered her eyes and took a long sip of her drink. Moments later, the waiter came with her order. I couldn't help but notice that the waiter, a perverted little white guy with a weird-looking goatee, seemed to be looking at the three of us for an extra long time, shifting his eyes from David to Jana and finally to me. It was clear that he considered me the third wheel - perhaps a chaperone or even Jana's father, for all I knew.

Yet he reserved his longest glances for my wife. As if he couldn't believe that David or I were with her. Like he was a little jealous of one or both of us. And all three of us noticed. At least that made Jana smile. As if she had no idea she could cause that kind of envy in men.

After the creepy waiter left, they picked out something at their dinners that I was sure I was paying for. Jana hates eating at normal times, so it was no surprise that she had no appetite before going upstairs and getting naked with a dark stranger.

The conversation didn't go well between them either. As if Jana didn't know what else to ask him. It seemed more like an interview than a flowing conversation. The whole thing felt like an awkward first date. Except there were three people sitting there. And two of them were practically guaranteed to have sex.

Just as things seemed to be stalling, Jana asked the question I knew had been burning in her mind since meeting this guy who showed up on her app, "Have you ever been with a white woman?"

The question obviously caught him off guard. Just as he was about to bite down on a forkful of rice. His hand shook and he dropped the rice right on his lap. It actually landed directly on his crotch, which was already bulging. Embarrassed, he looked down and then at Jana.

And I just knew what was going to happen.

This was a deal-breaker for Jana. She hated sloppy people. Any stain on a piece of clothing meant it had to be removed. That's one of her crazy behaviors.

I almost felt sorry for the guy. He was so close to screwing up. To nailing my wife.

But he couldn't close the deal. Too bad for him. Maybe Jana would be so disappointed after getting so turned on that she might even come to her husband for comfort sex.

I grabbed my napkin and wiped my mouth in
anticipation of an awkward but imminent departure.

Then my heart sank.

They locked eyes.

Jana giggled. She assured him it was no big deal. " Don't
worry about it. I'll get it for you," she said, picking up a
cocktail napkin and reaching under the table toward his
crotch.

What the heck?

It was so out of character for her. She would never think
of doing anything remotely inappropriate in public. But
I could practically see the excitement and desire
coursing through her body. As if this was what she had
been secretly and desperately waiting for, a chance to
touch a big black man in an intimate way.

Gently, she placed the napkin on his bulging crotch.
Even I could tell he was hard. She pressed the napkin

between her fingers to pick up the mischievous grains of rice. Only her fingers framed the outline of his shaft.

Even after scooping up the rice, she let her hand linger on his shaft. Then she squeezed his hard cock and looked into his eyes. He beamed at her boldness, but he certainly enjoyed it.

We were in a public restaurant. Everyone could see what she was doing. But she didn't seem to mind.

My eyes met those of a woman at another table. She was a little older than Jana, but pretty in her own way. She was with a man I assumed was her husband, whose head was buried in the menu. And she had seen the whole thing.

It took my breath away. I looked at my wife and silently begged her to stop. The last thing I wanted was for the manager to come over and make a scene.

I was so stunned as I stared at my wife's face. Her lips were parted and her tongue stuck out to wet them. She had a seductive look in her eyes as if she was overcome with the urge to pull down his zipper, grab his cock and start pumping it in and out of her mouth.

It was as if she had forgotten that we were in a public restaurant. As if her burning desire made the whole world around her disappear. Including her husband.

Finally, just before I reached out and pulled her hand away myself, she came back to her senses. She quickly scanned the restaurant to make sure no one was looking at her. The woman at the other table averted her gaze just before Jana noticed.

And even then, she gave his crotch one last squeeze before pulling her hand away and innocently leaning back as if none of this had ever happened.

As humiliated as I was, I realized that I was also hard. So hard that it was causing me pain and I had to move in my seat.

David stared at her for a few moments. It was as if he had never been with a woman like Jana - so beautiful, bold and eager to please her. He was mesmerized. Infatuated.

Jana had a powerful effect on him, and she knew it. It was obvious that he was attracted to her, and any reservations she may have had about the whole thing seemed to melt away.

The woman at the other table was watching us again. Well, maybe not all of us. She didn't notice me staring back. She had her eyes on Jana and what she was doing with David. Maybe she had her own ideas that didn't include the jerk of a husband.

The sexual arousal was practically emanating from my wife. It was like she was vibrating with desire. It went far beyond anything she had ever shown me, so I knew she would not be able to contain herself much longer. She no longer had an appetite for her dinner. She was hungry for this young stud's big black cock.

I excused myself from the table and tracked down our creepy waiter. I caught him whispering to one of his staff and nodding toward our table. He hadn't seen me coming and abruptly broke off his conversation when I asked him for the check. Jana was ready to go. Ready to go and ready to offer her body to David. And I didn't want to miss a beat.

I grabbed my receipt and headed back to our table. And I was shocked once again. My wife's hand was on his thigh and started rubbing it. David was sitting in the back of the alcove like a boss. He looked down and smiled as her hand slid onto his crotch. Just like before, she squeezed it and bit her lower lip. But that wasn't enough. She began to stroke the outline of his cock through his pants. Everyone could see it!

As I made it to the table, I glanced at the other woman who had seen the whole thing. She scowled at me, perhaps because I was blocking her view. She leaned toward her unsuspecting husband, and then something occurred to me. My wife could very well be responsible for two men having sex tonight. Unfortunately, neither of them was likely her husband.

"I think we should get out of here," Jana said.

"Aren't you going to eat?" he asked. He looked around the restaurant. He didn't seem worried that Jana would change her mind. He seemed to know she was a sure thing. Maybe he was just making her wait for it.

Jana answered him by sliding to his side of the alcove and taking his chin in her hands. She kissed him firmly on the mouth while her hand dipped back under the table. That was enough to convince him it was time to go.

" Did you get a room?" he asked.

She bit her lip and reached into her dress over her large breasts that were practically falling out. "Yes."

During the five-minute elevator ride to the room, they couldn't stop tugging at each other's clothes. Even when there were other people in the elevator. An older man, with his wife by his side, couldn't resist sneaking glances at them. They were like two wild animals pawing at each other, ready to mate. They pawed and scratched, grunted and moaned.

By the time the elevator reached our floor, they were both panting and out of breath. As we got off, Jana's shoulder strap slipped down and her big bare chest popped out. She didn't seem to notice until David's big black hand clasped it. He thumped the hard nipple with his thumb. Jana threw her head back, and I swear she spread her legs right there in the hallway.

Another couple came around the corner and stopped short, eyes wide and jaws splayed. I was horrified and cleared my throat.

David smiled and straightened my wife out as he slid the clothes strap back into place. Jana's bare chest was once again covered.

The couple walked awkwardly past and entered the elevator. As the doors closed, they began to laugh, and the man said, "Get a room."

The hotel room key card fell out of Jana's hand and slid across the carpet. I grabbed it and led her down the hall to the double doors of the suite, which I unlocked and opened for her as if I were a bellhop. I did everything but hold out my hand for my tip.

Under normal circumstances, I would have been thrilled with the suite. The double doors opened to an elevated foyer. Then down two steps to a luxurious living room with gilded sofas that framed a view of the city at night that was worth the not insignificant nightly price. The doors to the separate master bedrooms opened on either side.

However, they didn't even make it into either bedroom. As soon as they stumbled over the threshold, they began ripping each other's clothes off. Jana fumbled with the buttons of his shirt, but he had no trouble reaching into her dress with greedy hands.

It was up to me to close the doors behind them so they didn't give the other guests any more of a show than they had already put on.

The big black man seemed especially eager to get at my wife's full breasts. Maybe they weren't as firm and perky as they used to be, but they had increased in size and were incredibly attractive in their own right. And he didn't seem to be complaining.

He pushed aside the sheer fabric and sucked hungrily on them, pressing his thick lips to her erect nipples. This attention made Jana moan with pleasure. She seemed incredibly aroused. Part of her problem with his shirt was the fact that one of her hands kept sliding under her dress and between her thighs.

I had never seen her like that before. It was as if she wanted nothing more than to have this big black stud's thick cock deep inside her tight pussy.

Suddenly she jumped out of her panties. In her excitement, her panties were completely soaked. He spun her around and pushed her back against the wall while I stepped in from behind and picked up her underwear. I couldn't help but bring them right up to my nose. I closed my eyes and breathed in her fresh floral scent.

They were totally into each other and paid no attention to me. So I just watched them as I slid my hand into my own pants. My cock throbbed and I reached out to do something. The sight of her in the arms of this young black stranger turned me on more than I ever thought possible.

While he sucked on her breasts, she undid his belt and
zipper. Her fists clutched a handful of fabric as she
pulled his khakis down to his knees. She shivered a little
as she reached into his boxer briefs and pulled out his
massive black cock. It was thick and full and dwarfed
her porcelain hand.

His hard cock was angled straight up toward her face,
practically begging to be sucked. She held it there,
staring at it, marveling at its size and power. It was an
image I'll remember as surely as if I'd taken a picture.

He reached for the straps on her shoulders and nudged
her sides. Her dress slid down until the straps caught in
the folds of her elbows. Finally, both her breasts swung
free. Her fair skin was already turning red and pink from
his rough treatment.

She dropped to her knees, her ruined dress crumpling
around her, and took his cock in her mouth. Just a taste
at first, as she flicked her tongue around the mushroom
head. She locked her eyes on his to better gauge his
reactions.

He smiled and nodded, and she began to blow the young black man. She was aggressive, like she wanted to get as much of his cock in her mouth as she could. Like she dared to give him a blowjob he would never forget. That would set her apart from all the other girls.

Jana worked her hand up and down his shaft, not unlike what I was doing to myself. With her other hand, she played with his asshole.

"Do you like it?" she asked in a breathy voice. "Do you like the way I suck your cock?" She waited for his answer, pushing his cock straight up and sucking and licking his balls.

The big black man moaned in response. He threw his head back and closed his eyes. Jana laughed at his response. Then she put two fingers in her mouth and coated them with her saliva. He looked down to see what she was up to.

She just gave him the sloppiest smile. So dirty that I had to stop jerking off to keep from coming right in my pants.

She told him to get out of his pants, which he did while she held his cock. Then she reached between his thighs and began rubbing saliva slick fingers around the rim of his asshole.

"Oh yeah, baby." He began to moan louder. Then she slid the first finger into his asshole. Followed by the second. "Oh fuck."

"You're not going to cum, are you?" said Jana as she pumped his asshole. "Because you're not allowed to cum yet. I'm not ready yet." My wife was half his size and she was playing with him. She had everything under control.

"Ohhhh, fuck," he said. "I don't know how much longer I can."

Jana continued to finger-fuck his asshole and stroke his cock until he began to spasm. She had taken him to the edge.

One thing I know, I had to give him credit, because he lasted a whole lot longer than I would have if she had done that to me. But of course, she never would have done that. The anal play was something we hadn't even thought about.

She pulled her fingers out of his ass, but continued to rub his cock lightly with both hands. Just enough to keep him right there on the edge.

While she looked up at him, obviously admiring David's athletic build, I tried to see what he had that I didn't. I mean, he had six-pack abs and huge muscular arms, and his thighs and calves didn't look too shabby either. Those were things I could theoretically work on. But his exotic dark skin? There was nothing I could do about that, except maybe get a tan now and then.

But the bottom line was literally his huge cock. I mean, seeing Jana on her knees practically worshipping him was almost too much. It was the one thing I could never compete with.

Jana dropped a hand under the rumpled dress between her thighs. It looked like she had to, like she couldn't resist the urge to have him inside her. She got up from her knees and left the dress on the floor.

Completely naked except for her wedding ring, she stood on her tiptoes and kissed him. They kissed deeply for a long time with open mouths and swirling tongues. Jana kept stroking his shaft. He lay against her belly and the head reached up between her large naked breasts.

He had to duck a little to place his oversized palm over her slender pussy. His long fingers curled underneath, forcing her to spread her thighs and coo in pleasure. He pulled his hand away, his fingers slick with her arousal. He brought them to his lips and tasted them before offering them for her to suck.

Then Jana took charge. She turned to one of the bedrooms and pulled him along his cock. "Follow me," she said with a saucy look over her shoulder. As if he had a choice. Besides, he was more than eager to lure her into a bedroom and have his way with my wife.

She glanced at me, and we made eye contact. That was it. She was going to let him fuck her. Eye contact was my last chance to say anything. Anything at all.

But no words came. My mouth was dry.

But that wasn't why I didn't object.

I wanted to watch her with him. I needed to watch my wife spread her legs for his big black cock. Nothing else mattered.

I followed them. The third wheel all the way.

When they got to the bedroom, Jana practically threw him on the bed, despite his size. She was the aggressor, enjoying her role as the dominant older woman over his athletic manhood.

She was the total opposite of the shy, innocent housewife I knew. At home, I always had to take the initiative. And by initiate, I mean beg for it. And it was the same every time. Missionary. Me upstairs while she looked at the ceiling. Until I finished and she retreated to the bathroom.

But with this big black man, she seemed to enjoy really being in control of a man in bed for the first time in her life.

And I fell in love all over again.

David played along willingly. He looked like a predator, always on the prowl. But with Jana in power, he was the prey.

So he lay down on his back. He seemed to have no problem being the submissive she forced him to be. For all his charm, athleticism and masculinity, the young, tall, black stallion had no problem letting my wife take control.

Jana wasted no time. She literally jumped on the bed with him and started straddling him. She pushed his cock down so she could slide along its length while gyrating her hips back and forth.

Then she took his hard cock in her hand and began rubbing it against her clit. Even from the side, I could see that her pussy was getting extremely wet.

But there was a problem.

A big one.

There was no way his huge cock would fit inside her.

It wasn't that long ago that she was complaining that I was hurting her, and honestly, my cock was barely half the size of his. Maybe not even that.

Jana, however, was not deterred. She simply closed her eyes and rocked back and forth. Finally, she couldn't take it any longer. She stilled the big, hard cock and slowly lowered herself. At first, nothing. Then the head of his cock popped into her.

Jana cried out, but held still. She clenched her fist and closed her eyes. After a moment, she took a deep breath and slid further down his shaft. Somehow he disappeared into her wet cunt, and she sighed with pleasure.

"Holy shit, you're so tight," David said. His voice was a ragged gasp. He shifted his gaze to me. "Are you sure you're not a virgin anymore?"

Jana laughed hard. Her breasts bounced as she did, and I felt humiliated. He was making fun of me while my wife was impaled on his monster cock.

"I've never been with anyone as big as you. You fill me up completely. My husband could never do that." She started riding his cock like an expert. She rose up to the head before plunging back down to his balls. And she began to speed up. She was going wild.

David licked his thick lips as he watched her bounce on him. He tried to control her by holding her hips, but her bucking was too much for him. All he could do was play with her tits.

"Ooh, your huge cock feels so good," she said as she held his hands to her chest. "So fucking good."

David's eyes were wide as he stared at her in ecstasy. As if no woman had ever ridden his cock like this before.

No wonder it wasn't long before he began to tense and clench, fighting off the urge to come. No doubt he didn't want to blow his load too quickly.

But Jana didn't notice. Or she didn't care. She kept riding him like it was a race. Her long hair flowed wildly as she rocked back and forth on him. She closed her eyes and began to moan louder.

At that moment, David lost his mind. He kicked his legs straight across the bed and let out a loud scream as he pumped his load into her cunt.

Jana's back arched as she leaned back. Her moans turned to cries of pleasure as her hand thrummed over her clit and she came with him. They both trembled as their passion exploded into each other.

Their movements gradually slowed until she collapsed in his arms, their bodies glistening with sweat. Jana's head rested on his chest. She smiled contentedly as she saw her young, black lover immobilized. He was completely exhausted.

She slowly lifted her ass and let his soft but still huge cock slide out of her. She angled herself so she could take his cock back into her mouth. Gently, she jerked it up and down a few times and swirled her tongue around the head. Then she began licking up and down the shaft.

David's whole body trembled with pleasure. His eyes were closed and he was still breathing deeply.

Jana finally left his cock alone and rolled off him onto her back. A drop of cum dripped from her gaping cunt.

She looked up at me and raised her eyebrows.

That was all the encouragement I needed. I tore off my clothes and practically jumped onto the bed.

The bouncing bed stirred David, who took one look at my naked body and said, "Oh, hell no."

He got his energy back and jumped to his feet. He grabbed his clothes and laughed as he jumped into the bathroom.

"So what do you want to do now?" I asked my wife. Warmth radiated from her warm skin. The scent of her passion overwhelmed me.

She looked at me and pointed to her crotch. She spread her legs in case I hadn't gotten the message.

David's load was still oozing out of her. "Seriously?" said I. Cleaning up his mess was not what I had in mind.

Jana propped herself up on her elbows. "Thomas, in case you haven't noticed, things are going to change between us. So you can do whatever you want. Just know that I need more from you than I've been getting so far..."

"Okay, okay. I get it." The last thing I wanted was an argument. What I wanted most was to be with my wife. No matter what.

She raised her eyebrows again, surprised this time.

If that's what she wanted, then that's what I would do. I didn't want to lose her.

Besides, I was hard as hell.

I grinded through between her spread thighs. The sweet aroma of her fucking did something to me. I closed my eyes and pressed my face to her cunt. I started running all over and cleaning, just like she had done minutes before with David.

That's when the bathroom door opened and I heard David laughing. Shame burned my cheeks. I started to lift my head, but Jana grabbed a handful of my hair and held me in place.

The laughter stopped.

"Oh, my mistake," David said.

I assumed Jana was silently scolding him.

"Thank you, David," Jana said. "And my husband thanks you, too." It wasn't like I would have been able to respond with my mouth buried in her cunt.

I opened my eyes and looked up at Jana. My view of her was obscured by her pussy and the underside of her breasts.

"It was my pleasure," David said.

"Maybe we can do it again sometime?" Jana took his hand.

"Sure thing, Jana." He leaned forward and they kissed. Then he said to me, "You're a lucky man, my friend. Take care of her." I heard David walk out of the bedroom and out of the suite.

I continued until Jana started bucking her hips in my face. She was breathing hard and her nipples were rock hard. When she came, she squeezed my head between her thighs.

As her orgasm began to subside, she pulled me up to kiss her. She reached down and stroked my cock as she guided it inside her.

I was so aroused that I barely lasted a minute. And when I was done, I collapsed on top of her. She stroked the back of my head and told me she loved me.

And she stared at the ceiling. She was probably thinking about her next date.

www.ingramcontent.com/pod-product-compliance
Lightning Source LLC
Chambersburg PA
CBHW051958150726
47999CB00004B/1430